"It's not like that," Williams interjected. "Normally Yamun is never seen . . . I mean *never* seen. Someone hears about him, perhaps security is tightened for no explainable reason someplace, and it means Yamun is probably in the area. But to actually photograph him, that means trouble."

"I still don't understand."

"Yamun, the Israelis think, is getting set to move. To pull something," Williams said.

"And this is how the man does it?" Carter asked incredulously. "He comes out in the open and damn near advertises the fact?"

NICK CARTER IS IT!

"Nick Carter out-Bonds James Bond."
—*Buffalo Evening News*

"Nick Carter is America's #1 espionage agent."
—*Variety*

"Nick Carter is razor-sharp suspense."
—*King Features*

"Nick Carter has attracted an army of addicted readers . . . the books are fast, have plenty of action and just the right degree of sex . . . Nick Carter is the American James Bond, suave, sophisticated, a killer with both the ladies and the enemy."
—*The New York Times*

FROM THE NICK CARTER KILLMASTER SERIES

THE ALGARVE AFFAIR
ASSIGNMENT: RIO
THE BLUE ICE AFFAIR
THE BUDAPEST RUN
CARIBBEAN COUP
CIRCLE OF SCORPIONS
DAY OF THE MAHDI
THE DEATH DEALER
DEATH HAND PLAY
DEATH ISLAND
THE DEATH STAR AFFAIR
THE DUBROVNIK MASSACRE
THE GOLDEN BULL
THE KREMLIN KILL
THE LAST SAMURAI
THE MACAO MASSACRE
THE MAYAN CONNECTION
NIGHT OF THE WARHEADS
NORWEGIAN TYPHOON

OPERATION SHARKBITE
THE PARISIAN AFFAIR
PURSUIT OF THE EAGLE
THE REDOLMO AFFAIR
REICH FOUR
RETREAT FOR DEATH
THE SATAN TRAP
SIGN OF THE COBRA
SOLAR MENACE
THE STRONTIUM CODE
THE SUICIDE SEAT
TIME CLOCK OF DEATH
TRIPLE CROSS
TURKISH BLOODBATH
THE VENGEANCE GAME
WAR FROM THE CLOUDS
THE YUKON TARGET
ZERO-HOUR STRIKE FORCE

NICK CARTER

KILLMASTER

THE VENGEANCE GAME

CHARTER BOOKS, NEW YORK

THE VENGEANCE GAME

A Charter Book/published by arrangement with
The Condé Nast Publications, Inc.

PRINTING HISTORY
Charter Original/May 1985

Charter Books are published by The Berkley Publishing Group,
200 Madison Avenue, New York, New York 10016.
PRINTED IN THE UNITED STATES OF AMERICA

Dedicated to the men of the
Secret Services of the
United States of America

PROLOGUE

It was early afternoon of a very warm day when the very fast Israeli Kfir fighter-bomber touched down at Lod Airport, just outside Tel Aviv, and the pilot expertly taxied across to the military section.

He was directed into a large hangar where he set the brakes and cut the switches. Even as his canopy was coming open and the big hangar doors were ponderously rumbling closed, two technicians from Aman—Israeli military intelligence—were unloading the high-speed film canisters from the belly of the plane.

The pilot, Captain Uri Mennen, unstrapped as his boarding ladder was trundled over, and he climbed down from the cockpit, handing his helmet to one of the other flight technicians.

No one said a word. None of them had any need to speak. They all had their orders.

Captain Mennen had been ordered to overfly a section of desert to the south of Tripoli in Libya and take a series of high-resolution photographs of a training compound there.

He was also ordered to stick with his film when he returned, personally escorting the canisters to the Aman photo-processing lab right there at the airport, and finally to bring the prints and the negatives to Aman headquarters downtown near the Histadrut Building, and a hundred yards from Mossad headquarters.

The technicians took the canisters out of the cameras, loaded them onto a pushcart, and hurried across the hangar, Captain Mennen directly behind them.

"Have some coffee, Captain. This will take a half hour," the photo lab chief, a burly Jew who had come from Chicago, said.

The canisters disappeared into the dark photo lab, and alone, Captain Mennen poured himself a cup of coffee in the day room and sat down by the window. He lit himself a cigarette as he stared out across the airport.

His flight had shown up on Libyan radar, of course, but before they could send up interceptors, or fire a missile, he was well offshore in the Mediterranean, making a wide, sweeping turn more than a hundred miles out.

A second pass brought him directly over his target, where he had keyed the cameras, and then he dropped like a supersonic stone well beneath Libyan radar, streaking back across the border and finally home.

It was a tactic they had been using to good effect just lately. Sooner or later the Libyans would get wise to what they were doing, and exactly why they were doing it, but for now it worked.

Captain Mennen thought about that, as well as of his wife and children. All this, naturally, was for them. Something very big was occurring in the Libyan desert. He did not know that directly, of course. No one told him. He did not have the need to know. But it was sufficient that he was overflying the country, taking photographs that were apparently very important, for him to understand something big was afoot.

Exactly twenty-nine minutes after the film canisters had gone into the lab, the chief brought the developed films back out, packed in two cardboard boxes.

He handed them to Captain Mennen with a nod. "These are really excellent shots, Captain," the chief said. "Really very good. They're going to be happy with you downtown.''

"Thanks," Mennen said. He took the boxes across the hangar where his escort—two armed men in civilian clothes—were waiting for him. Together they climbed into an unmarked Buick sedan, and the driver took off immediately.

Within twenty minutes they were pulling into the driveway of a very plain four-story building downtown that ostensibly housed the military acquisitions section. Around back their driver parked near the door, and Captain Mennen, carrying the film, hurried into the building and up to the fourth floor, where he was ushered immediately into the office of Major General David Lapides, head of Aman.

"Ah, Mennen, here you are," Lapides said.

Three other men were in the large office with the Aman chief: a photo analyst, Lapides's number-two man, and Aharon Levi, the chief liaison with the Israeli secret service, the Mossad.

"Was there any trouble with the Libyan Air Force?" Lapides asked.

"No, sir, none whatsoever," Mennen said. He opened the two cartons. One contained the prints, the second the negatives. He spread the photos out across a long conference table that had been set up for just this meeting.

The photographs showed the compound in the Libyan desert in startling detail. Some of them were so good, the light just right, that even the insides of the buildings could be made out through the windows.

"Here," Lapides said, stabbing a finger at a face in one of the pictures. It was the back garden of the main building. A dozen men sat around a swimming pool. One of them was looking up directly into the camera as if he knew that he was being photographed, and he wanted to make sure the camera caught him fullface.

"Is it him?" Levi, the Mossad liaison, asked.

"Yes, definitely," Lapides said.

"Just as we suspected."

"What are you telling me, Aharon?" Lapides snapped. "Is the mad dog off and running again? Is that it? Is that what we have to look forward to?"

Levi shrugged. He looked at the others with them in the room. "Perhaps we should be alone for this."

Lapides dismissed the others. "I would like you to remain, Captain Mennen," he said.

The others left. Mennen had no idea why he had been singled out to remain. Lapides answered it for him.

"I have two questions for you," he said. "This is, as you may have guessed, vitally important to us."

"Yes, sir," Mennen said uncertainly.

"Do you know who this man is in the photograph?"

"No, sir."

"His name is Abd-el Yamun. He was the mastermind of the massacre of our young people at the Olympics in Munich in 1972."

Mennen went cold. He could feel his muscles tightening.

"It was his first important accomplishment," Lapides continued. "Believe me when I tell you he has done a lot more since then."

"And he will continue," Levi said.

"I could load my plane, go back right now, and bomb him. He would be dead."

"It won't be that easy. Believe me in that as well. You flew over once. They know you were there. They know who you were. They would not let you get within ten miles of the compound now. Even if Yamun was still there—which I doubt he is," Lapides said.

"Why are you telling me this, sir?" Mennen asked.

Lapides smiled indulgently. "To impress upon you, Captain, the importance of your next answers."

Mennen was impressed.

"The first thing I would like to know is, did you notice anything unusual during your flyover? Anything at all? Even the slightest thing?"

"I don't know, sir. There was nothing. I flew across, made

my turn, and then came back for the photo run."

"And afterward?"

"I dropped to below their radar screen and came home."

"You were not chased?"

"No, sir."

"You were picked up on their radar?"

"Yes, sir. Coming in and out."

"No electronic interference of any kind?" Levi asked.

"No, sir," Mennen replied, turning to the Mossad liaison chief. "My ECM equipment was quiet, except for the radar pulses."

"I see," Levi said. He turned back to Lapides. "I would have thought they'd have done something more to protect Yamun."

"This could have been a spur-of-the-moment meeting."

"It could be nothing. Perhaps he was simply on holiday."

"I cannot believe that," Lapides said sharply. He looked again at the photographs. "One last question, Captain, and then you can go."

"Sir?"

"Is there any possibility, even the slightest chance, that these photographs could have been tampered with?"

"No, sir," Mennen said. "They never left my sight except for when they were in the photo lab. And the chief himself was there processing them. Alone."

"That's it, then," Lapides said to Levi. "We'll have to assume that the bloody bastard is up to something again." He looked at the photos. "Something big, I'd guess, looking at the size of the group he's got there."

"But there were no protective measures around him," Levi protested.

"Maybe he's coming out. Maybe he's getting used to operating without all the paraphernalia of watchdogs around him."

Levi shrugged and got his jacket from where it was draped over a chair. "I'll get back now. I'll inform Esterman."

"The CIA liaison?" Lapides asked. "Why him?"

"They've been a big help to us with Yamun. Maybe they'll have something to add. Maybe they'll have a suggestion."

"Pardon me, sir," Mennen said. He was truly confused now.

Lapides turned to him. "Yes?"

"I don't understand, sir. Why don't we just kill the bastard and get it over with?"

Levi and Lapides exchanged glances. "What do you think we've been trying to do all these years?"

"Is he that tough, sir?"

"And then some," Levi said. "And then some."

ONE

Nick Carter was a tall man with a powerful build, but he had an easy, athletic grace that was obvious even to the most casual observer. His eyes, when he was upset, became almost black, and the set of his jaw was resolute.

It was a warm midsummer Sunday when he entered Washington, D.C., from the north. All week the weather across the Eastern Seaboard had been gorgeous. On Friday, Carter had driven up to Atlantic City, where he had relaxed at one of the casinos with an old friend who had flown in from Rome to be with him.

Marielle Rossini and Carter went back quite a few years. He had met her on an assignment that had taken him to Sicily. She had been married at the time to a Mafia bigwig who later was gunned down in Palermo.

For a time he and Marielle had been a thing. Each of them had used each other, and both of them knew it, Carter for the information he could get about Mafia activities from her, and she because she enjoyed living dangerously.

He lit one of his custom-made cigarettes, his initials embossed in gold on the filter, and merged with the light Sunday traffic on the Baltimore-Washington Parkway. He drove with the top down on his restored Jaguar XKE, the warm wind and sun wonderful.

They had played blackjack and made love all weekend, but last night Marielle had told him their thing was over.

"I am to be married again, Nicholas," she had told him in Italian. She spoke English very well, but when they were together, especially when they made love, they spoke Italian. The language was softer, more musical than English, somehow more suitable.

"Another Cosa Nostra guy?" Carter had asked. He lay propped up in the wide bed on the top floor of the casino-hotel. Marielle, nude, had just stepped out of the bathroom. She poured herself a glass of champagne, then came over to the bed.

"It will not do for me to associate with you, *il mio amore*."

"No?" Carter asked. "Are you going to leave me this minute?" It was just before midnight.

Marielle smiled broadly. She was a sultry, dark-haired beauty with high cheekbones, delicate features, lovely, well-formed breasts, a slightly rounded tummy, and a marvelous technique.

"No," she said. "I will leave tomorrow. Tonight . . ." She let it trail off.

"Tonight is still ours?"

She was still smiling when she got into bed with Carter, and without warning she slowly poured the ice-cold champagne over his chest, his stomach, and the tops of his legs.

Carter willed himself not to react.

Marielle tossed her empty glass aside and came to Carter, kissing and licking his chest, and slowly working her way downward. "I love champagne this way," she said languorously.

Carter had to smile thinking about the previous night. That morning he had gone down to the coffee shop for breakfast, and by the time he returned, she was gone. No note, nothing. But it was typical of her. He figured he'd be seeing her again in a couple of years. Either her new husband would get assassinated in some gangland dispute, or she would get tired of him and break it off.

The parkway became New York Avenue, which led past the White House. There were quite a few tourists in town today, maybe one in a thousand understanding what real power was wielded here in this town. They saw pretty buildings and statues, but not the real corridors of power.

He cut across on Pennsylvania Avenue and then went up to Georgetown where he'd recently purchased an apartment in a row of exquisitely restored brownstones. He turned down his street, passed his place, and parked his car in the garage he rented around the corner.

He took his single bag out of the back, locked up the garage, walked back to his building, and went upstairs.

His mind was not really on anything but the pleasant afternoon and the remembrances of the soft touch of Marielle Rossini, so he did not notice anything but some children playing down the street and a bus stopping at the corner in the opposite direction until he got to his door.

He smelled after shave lotion. It was very strong.

For a good number of years now, Carter had worked for an organization called AXE, ostensibly a supersecret intelligence service arm of the State Department but in truth a nearly autonomous action-oriented agency. Any job that was too messy for the CIA, too difficult for the National Security Agency, or too risky for the military intelligence services fell under presidential order to AXE.

Carter was very highly placed within this organization that was fronted by Amalgamated Press and Wire Services on Dupont Circle. So highly placed that he carried the N3 designation. He was, in the vernacular, licensed to kill. And he was an expert.

He set his bag down in the corridor, pulled out the 9mm Luger he always carried, and very carefully tried the door. It was unlocked.

Easing the door open, Carter stepped in sideways, presenting less of a target. Over the years in his business he had built up quite a collection of enemies. It could be any one of them now.

The odor of after shave lotion was even stronger now that the door was open. But Carter could see no one inside.

He slipped in, the safety catch on Wilhelmina, his Luger off, a round in the chamber. At the corner of the end of the short corridor, he flattened himself against the wall.

"Oh, do come in, Carter," a man said from inside.

Carter laughed out loud despite himself. "You could get yourself killed that way, Williams," he said, holstering the gun and stepping around the corner.

Brad Williams, who described himself as a damned Connecticut Yankee but in actuality was from London, and who worked the Far East desk at AXE headquarters, sat in the easy chair by the front window, his legs crossed. The entire apartment reeked of after shave lotion.

"Did you pick my lock, or did Housekeeping give you the key?" Carter asked. He stepped back out into the corridor, got his bag, and walked to the window. Williams had gotten to his feet.

"No time to chat, friend Nicholas. Mount Olympus calls."

"Hawk?"

Williams's manner suddenly became serious. "He sent me around to fetch you. And yes, I did get your key from Housekeeping, although I had to practically sign my life away to get it. Bastards."

Carter chuckled, his manner outwardly light, but inside his gears were churning. David Hawk, the hard-bitten chief of AXE, went way back in this business. He had never taken anything lightly in his life—not even as a child, so the stories went—and Carter could believe it.

Over the years he and Hawk had built up a close relationship, almost that of a father and son, except that their deep mutual respect had been earned, not inherited.

It was a Sunday. Normally Hawk would have waited until Carter showed up on the officer of the day's desk on Monday.

(It was a job Carter was assigned between field missions. He hated it.) Or in an important case, Hawk would have telephoned. But to send someone in person for him, something big was definitely in the works.

Carter tossed his bag in his bedroom, splashed some cold water on his face, then followed Williams downstairs.

"We'll just take the company's transportation," Williams said as a plain blue Chevrolet Caprice pulled up.

He and Carter climbed in the back seat, and the driver took off immediately.

"Any hints from upstairs?" Carter asked, settling back and lighting a cigarette.

"Oh, do you really have to?" Williams asked, eyeing the curling smoke.

"Yes," Carter said.

"We've got some sort of tickle from the Mossad. Burt Esterman passed it along earlier today."

"Any idea what it's about?"

Williams looked at Carter. "Actually, yes, but Hawk would deep-six me if he knew I was talking. Everyone is walking on tippytoes around there."

Carter settled back with his own thoughts. Something definitely big and probably very nasty had come up. But what? From the dailies he had been looking at during the past few weeks, everything was quiet in that part of the world.

AXE was housed on Dupont Circle in the Amalgamated Press and Wire Services Building, so it only took them a couple of minutes to make it there from Georgetown.

They pulled around back and down into the underground parking ramp beneath the building. The driver left them off by the elevator, and they went upstairs, first to the duty room and then by private elevator to Hawk's office.

His secretary was expecting them. She buzzed Hawk. "Mr. Williams and N3 are here, sir."

"Fine, send them in," Hawk's voice rasped.

Carter and Williams went into Hawk's cluttered office.

"The O.D. said you had left the city for the weekend

without logging out," Hawk said, taking his half-chewed cigar out of his mouth. He was a short man with thick white hair and a gruff manner.

"I went to Atlantic City, sir," Carter said.

"I know where you were, Nick. What I want to know is why you felt you did not have to log out."

"My time is my own, sir," Carter said. Williams stopped in midstride.

Hawk chuckled. "After this, leave us a note. When they come after you, I want to know where you are so that we can at least try to help you."

"Yes, sir," Carter said.

Hawk waved him and Williams to chairs opposite the desk. When they were settled, Carter lit another cigarette.

"This is a tough one," Hawk began.

Carter could feel his blood begin to race. He hated desk work. The very worst field assignment was much better than the very best office job.

"Sir?" he said.

"How do you feel? Are you fit?"

"Yes, sir."

Hawk opened a folder on his desk and glanced at its contents. He extracted a couple of photos and handed them over to Carter. "These are a few years old."

They were both of a man, obviously an Arab. In one instance the man was dressed in battle fatigues, his eyes averted from the camera's lens. He carried a Soviet Kalashnikov assault rifle. It looked as if he were under fire. The second photo was of the same man, only this time he was in a bathing suit and lounging beside a pool that was in the desert somewhere. There were guards in traditional Arab dress on the high walls surrounding the pool.

Carter looked up. "Lebanon—perhaps Libya?"

"Just outside Beirut in that one, and within Beirut in the first," Hawk said. "Have you any idea who the man is?"

Carter studied the photographs again, something tugging at his memory. It was something from years ago, he thought.

The man in the pictures was large and very well built. In the poolside photograph his muscles were plainly visible, as were a number of scars—some old, some new—and several were obviously from gunshot wounds.

"No, sir, I can't quite place him. It looks as if he's been around, though."

"Yes," Hawk said dryly. He nodded toward Williams. "Tell him."

"His name is Abd-el Yamun," Williams began. "He was born in Palestine, and for a time he fought with Arafat. But since the Munich Olympics—"

Carter cut him off. "Yamun, yes! He was the mastermind behind that business."

"One and the same," Williams said. "He's been quite busy since then as well. As have Israeli intelligence, the German BND, Interpol, and the intelligence and police services of a dozen countries, trying to catch up with him."

"A single bullet in the head shouldn't be all that difficult."

"Don't underestimate this man, Nick," Hawk said. "For at least ten years, some of the best cops in the Middle East and Europe have been trying to do just that."

"There is a string of dead law enforcement agents from London to Tel Aviv and back," Williams said.

Carter looked again at the photographs, this time with much more respect and a rising curiosity. *Is he that good?* he wondered.

Williams continued. "For the past four years, as far as we know, Yamun has been working directly for Colonel Muammar Qaddafi. Libya is his permanent free goal. Once there, no one can touch him."

"Every Libyan embassy or consulate is his bolt-hole, then," Carter said.

"Exactly," Williams said. "He can pop out, strike, and jump back into his rabbit hole where no one else can follow him."

"That thing not so long ago in London—at the Libyan embassy—that wasn't him?"

"No," Hawk said. "Much too small for Yamun. He only concerns himself with big, dramatic actions."

Carter shook his head. "There hasn't been much happening lately. Not since the Marine barracks in Beirut . . ."

"That was his doing," Hawk said. "But you are correct; nothing much has been happening just lately. So the Israelis have gotten, understandably, just a little nervous."

"I suppose he's their prize?"

"Just like Eichmann. They'll take all the help they can get, but when it comes to the kill, he's their property."

"Understandable after Munich," Carter said. "But it doesn't sound like they're doing much of a job of it."

"They're worried just now that he's on his way out again," Williams said.

"The Mossad spotted him outside of Tripoli and handed the job of a once-in-and-once-out photo reconnaissance mission to their military intelligence branch."

"Aman."

"Yes," Hawk said. "They came back with positive proof that Yamun was there, outside of Tripoli, in a meeting with a number of other known terrorist planners and leaders."

Carter shrugged. "So what?" he asked. "Libya is the man's home. Why wouldn't he be seen there?"

"It's not like that," Williams interjected. "Normally Yamun is never seen . . . I mean *never* seen. Someone hears about him, perhaps security is tightened for no explainable reason someplace, and it means Yamun is probably in the area. But to actually photograph him, that means trouble."

"I still don't understand."

"Yamun, the Israelis think, is getting set to move. To pull something," Williams said.

"And this is how the man does it?" Carter asked incredulously. "He comes out in the open and damn near advertises the fact?"

Hawk sat back in his chair. "The man is arrogant," he said.

"He can't be stupid as well," Carter said. "Not and have eluded capture all this time."

"You're right, of course," Hawk said. "It was only happenstance, from what we understand, that the Israelis spotted him. But they think it's significant that Yamun was meeting with other terrorist planners in a Qaddafi compound. It was because of the others that the Israelis were able to get the photographs. On his own, running his own operation, they'd never have spotted him."

Carter had finished his cigarette. He lit another. "So now what, sir?" he asked. "Are the Israelis asking for our help? They think Yamun is going to break out and do something nasty?"

"That's exactly what they're asking for," Hawk said.

"But simply help in running Yamun to ground? When it comes to the nitty-gritty, they'll back our man off?"

"They want him in one piece so that he can stand trial in Israel."

"Let Esterman handle it. He's already liaison over there."

"He's CIA, and he does not carry a Killmaster designation," Hawk said, his normally gruff voice very soft, menacing.

Williams sucked in his breath. The butterflies and tight feeling that had been building in Carter's gut suddenly loosened. There was more to this than met the eye.

"I have your attention, I see," Hawk said.

"Yes, sir."

"This will not only be a tough assignment, it will be a very delicate one."

Carter held his silence.

"I want you over in Tel Aviv by morning, as a CIA operative. You will ostensibly be coming in to help Esterman deal with the Israelis on this one. Give them whatever they want and need. If they want a messenger boy, then you'll become a messenger boy. Whatever, you'll do it. Make them happy."

Williams seemed a little uncomfortable. Carter continued to hold his peace.

"In the meantime, you will gather whatever information you can in addition to what you'll be given before you leave here. Sooner or later Yamun will get out of Libya, and the Israelis will be going after him. You'll tag along if at all possible."

"And if it's not possible, sir? If the Israelis leave me behind?"

"Then you're on your own, Nick. I've spoken with the President about this, and he agrees with me. We want no publicity, but we do want Yamun dead. After all, they were our Marines in Beirut."

"You want me to find him and kill him," Carter said.

Williams had shrunk back a little.

Hawk nodded.

"What if the Israelis get in my way? What if they try to stop me?"

Hawk took a very long time to answer, and when he did it was obvious he was choosing his words with great care.

"It will be far too dangerous to try and capture the man alive. In that there can be no argument. If you get close enough to him to kill him, then do not hesitate. If anyone gets in your way . . . you will have to use your own judgment. Whatever happens—*whatever*—you will not be left out in the cold. We will back you."

A chill played up Carter's spine. The Israelis were friends. But Yamun had killed so many people, had done so much damage, and caused so much grief and suffering, that getting him transcended even friendship.

"Yes, sir," Carter said.

For a long moment no one moved. Finally, however, Hawk closed the file folder in front of him and handed it across to Carter.

"I can't let you take this with you, but there is some interesting reading to bring you up-to-date. Williams will help on that score as well."

Carter and Williams got to their feet.

"When do you want me out of here?" Carter asked.

"You're scheduled on the TWA overnight to Paris, and from there direct to Tel Aviv on El Al. Esterman will be waiting for you."

Carter looked at his watch. It was after four. He still had a few hours before he had to be out at the airport.

He and Williams went to the door, but another thought struck Carter and he turned back.

Hawk was staring at him, a pensive look in his eyes.

"Sir?"

Hawk nodded.

"Yamun doesn't work alone, does he?"

"Not to our knowledge. At least he hasn't in the past, and from what Esterman says about the photographs taken by the recon plane, he was in with a group of planners this time as well."

"But he gets involved in the actual operations themselves?" Carter asked. "I mean he's actually there on the scene? He's a triggerman as well as the planner?"

Again Hawk nodded. "What are you driving at, Nick?"

"Just this, sir," Carter said. "If I do get to the man, and I do manage to kill him in the middle or even at the beginning of whatever he's got planned, what's to prevent, let's say, one of his lieutenants from completing whatever it was they planned?" Carter glanced at Williams, then back. "I understand that the man is arrogant, but I cannot believe that he's stupid. He must know that he will be nailed sooner or later. And he must plan for that eventuality on each assignment. So what happens if I eliminate him too soon to know and therefore stop whatever it is they've got planned?"

Hawk's eyebrows knitted. He shook his head. "I can't answer that for you, N3. The man is dangerous. Do not turn down any chance to kill him."

"Yes, sir," Carter said.

"Good luck," Hawk called after them, and Carter and Williams went out the door.

Carter didn't really hear him, though. He was muttering half under his breath, "There are chances, and then there are chances."

TWO

The sun burned harshly on the main east-west runway of Lod Airport to the southeast of Tel Aviv as the El Al airliner touched down for a perfect landing. Nick Carter was tired from his hurried preparations the day before in Washington, D.C., and then the Washington-Paris overnight flight, and finally that morning's flight. He had not gotten much sleep, although he had rested with his eyes closed.

He kept thinking about Yamun. He kept seeing the man's cold eyes in the one photograph. It had struck Carter that there was no human warmth in the man's eyes. He knew that death and destruction meant little or nothing to Yamun. Only the goals it might accomplish meant anything. For Yamun, there was no such thing as the sanctity of human life.

Burt Esterman, the CIA liaison with the Mossad and Aman in Tel Aviv, was waiting just outside Customs when Carter was passed through. He was a tall man, somewhat on the thin side, with what appeared to be a permanent smirk on his lips. His eyes were narrow, and his hairline receded.

"Welcome to the unholy land," Esterman said, shaking Carter's hand. "How was your trip?"

"Long," Carter said.

Williams had worked with Esterman some years ago. He had warned Carter that the man was a jerk, with an inflated sense of his own importance.

"I have a room at the Sheraton for you. Didn't think you'd want to stay at the embassy," Esterman was saying.

Carter followed him across the terminal and outside, where he tossed his bags in the back seat of a ten-year-old Mercedes sedan. The car was in very good shape. Obviously Esterman took a great pride in it.

"I'm supposed to speak with David Lapides sometime this afternoon, is that right?"

Esterman looked at him. "Whatever for?"

"I'm to be briefed."

Esterman smiled faintly and shook his head. "Not necessary, Carter. I'll take care of all the little details. I just want you to tag along and keep a very low profile."

Hawk had said not to make waves. But he could not work in a vacuum. He was going to have to have a hell of a lot more freedom, and a certain amount of autonomy, right from the beginning.

"I hate to be the one to break this to you, Burt, but I've come over here to work *with* you, not *for* you. Now, you can set up a meeting with Lapides for me, or I'll do it myself."

Esterman puffed up. "See here, Carter . . ."

Carter lit a cigarette and looked away, totally tuning the man out. Esterman would complain to his bureau chief at the embassy, who in turn might complain back to the deputy director of Operations at Langley. The word might get up to the DCI, who would speak with Hawk, and that would be the end of that. Carter had his orders. They did not include holding Esterman's hand.

It took a half hour to get all the way into Tel Aviv and then across town to the Sheraton, which overlooked the Mediterranean. All during that time Esterman kept up a running commentary about how much he hated Tel Aviv, Israel, the Arabs *and* the Jews, and everything, in fact, that had anything to do with the Middle East.

"Sooner or later they're all going to blow each other to hell," the CIA liaison man said. "The Israelis have nukes, and once the Syrians get them—or, God forbid, if Qaddafi gets the bomb—this place will be kaput . . . oil and all.''

Carter turned to him. ''Is that what they're worried about?''

''What?''

''The bomb. Do the Israelis think that Yamun is going to get Libya a bomb?''

''An intriguing thought,'' Esterman said. ''But I don't think so. From what Lapides and Levi—he's my contact with the Mossad—say, Yamun's style is more toward straight out-and-out terrorism. Spectacular terrorism, but just gangland stuff after all. The bomb would be too big, I think.''

They pulled up beneath the canopy at the Sheraton, and Esterman started to get out of the car, but Carter stopped him.

''I'll see myself in. Just set up a meeting with Lapides—and with Levi, your Mossad man. This afternoon if possible.''

Esterman just looked at him for a moment. ''Who the hell do you think you are, coming in here like this, all high and mighty?''

Carter shook his head and smiled. ''Believe me, Burt, you don't want to know. Just set up the meeting like a good boy.'' He got out of the car, grabbed his bags from the back, and went into the hotel without bothering to look back.

The reservations were in his name. He was listed as an importer/exporter in Tel Aviv on business. He was shown up to a room on the fifth floor that overlooked the water, and after the bellman had gone, Carter took a long hot shower and ordered up a sandwich and a couple of bottles of cold beer.

While he waited for room service he unpacked his luggage, including the large, complicated-looking cassette recorder in which he carried his weapons through airport security measures.

The back of the recorder opened, and then the main printed circuit board lifted out. From within, Carter drew out Wilhelmina, his 9mm Luger, a silencer, and a couple of extra clips of ammunition. From a second slot he took out Hugo, his pencil-thin, razor-sharp stiletto in its chamois sheath.

From a final compartment he took out Pierre, a tiny gas bomb, highly effective and very deadly in close quarters.

His Luger went under his left armpit, his stiletto on his right forearm, and the gas bomb high on his inner thigh, almost like a third testicle.

He felt much more comfortable armed, although he understood that the Israeli authorities might take a dim view of his arsenal.

He dressed in a lightweight khaki desert outfit and soft boots, then called down to the front desk.

"This is Carter in five-oh-three. Are there any messages?"

"No, sir."

"Thank you. If someone tries to reach me, please take his name and number. I'm tired now, and I'm going to take a nap for a few hours. I don't wish to be disturbed."

"Of course, sir," the desk clerk said.

Carter hung up, checked in the mirror to make sure his Luger wasn't bulging noticeably, then left his room, getting off the elevator on the first floor and walking down the back stairs from the mezzanine so that no one at the front desk would see him leaving the hotel.

He walked around to the front of the hotel and caught a cab just coming up the driveway before it got to the front entrance. It was a short ride over to the downtown Hertz office where he leased a new Fiat convertible that came complete with a road map and a lengthy set of instructions outlining exactly what areas within Israel and the Sinai the car could be driven to and still have the insurance remain in effect.

Israel was, and always had been, a country under siege.

Within twenty minutes he was on the seacoast highway past the Sede Dov Airport toward Haifa, the traffic moderately heavy. He had put the top down, and although the sun was very hot and the wind more like the breath of a blast furnace than the refreshing breeze from an open car, Carter enjoyed it. It had been a very long winter.

He passed Herzhvyam and Netanya, both small towns on

the coast, before he turned inland to the Shomeron, the highways becoming progressively narrower and bumpier, and the temperature higher and higher the farther he went.

In the jacket Hawk had provided him with, Carter had noticed that at the time of the Munich massacre, Peri Sharon had been head of the special Mossad task force that had gone after Yamun.

Sharon had come very close to catching up with the Arab terrorist. He had had the man in his gunsights, one eyewitness had reported. But a bomb had gone off, and Sharon had been critically injured.

He had spent twenty-seven months in the hospital, the doctors putting his body back together piece by piece as best they could.

Sharon's career was over, of course. He was lucky to have come out of the encounter alive. After he had been released from the hospital, he had spent five years recuperating at a kibbutz, Gan Har 'Evm, about twenty-five miles inland.

The last entry in the AXE brief indicated that Sharon had elected to remain at the kibbutz and was now its manager.

There would not be many people in Israel who would be willing to talk to an American about Yamun . . . at least not openly. The Mossad and Aman certainly would not be very willing to give Carter the information he needed to track the terrorist.

But a man like Sharon, someone who had come so close and yet had missed, could possibly still harbor a grudge. Perhaps it would be strong enough to transcend national boundaries.

Sharon, Carter had figured from the start, would be his only hope of any real information—of at least any real initial information. Once he had a start, he figured he could carry it from there.

The narrowing roads led up into the hills, the groves of citrus trees giving way to the gnarled olive orchards that seemed able to thrive on any hot, arid hillside.

It was still early when Carter negotiated the last turn in the final dirt track that led down into a narrow valley in which the Gan Har 'Evm kibbutz was located.

The main gate was at the southern end of the valley, and within a couple of minutes of spotting it below, Carter was driving across the central square to the administration building.

He shut off the car, and the heat of the day hit him with its smothering intensity as he got out. Almost instantly he was drenched with sweat. He had forgotten what this part of the world was like.

A young woman in shorts, a T-shirt and no bra, with thick wool socks and heavy, short boots on her feet, came out of the administration building. When she spotted Carter she came over.

"It's not too often we get an American out here," she said with a big smile. Her accent was strictly New York.

Carter laughed. "Is it that obvious?"

"For me it is," the young woman said. She stuck out her hand. "Katy Shwartz. Brooklyn."

"Nick Carter. Washington," Carter said, shaking her hand.

"As in District of Columbia. You're with the government. And you're here to see Peri."

"You're psychic, too."

" 'Too'? What 'too'?"

"And pretty."

She laughed. "Tell me you've come to take me away from all this."

"I've come to see Mr. Sharon. But how did you know that?"

She shrugged. "He's had a lot of visitors over the past couple of days. It's the Munich thing. I guess the mad dog is breaking out again."

"Excuse me?"

"Yamun. He's known as the mad dog . . . ever since Munich."

Carter nodded his understanding. If everyone knew that

Yamun was on the way out and was being looked for, so would Yamun himself, which was going to make him a very dangerous adversary.

The young woman read something of that in Carter's eyes. "Come on in, Mr. Carter. I'll see if he'll talk to you. You with the CIA or something?"

"Or something," Carter said. He followed Katy into the administration center, which was housed in a long, low building with a corrugated metal roof. Just inside was the orderly room with a half-dozen desks, a large survey chart of the kibbutz, and a big map of Israel and the surrounding territory showing in various colors the various borders, depending upon which war established them.

"Just wait here a sec," Katy said, and she went down a short corridor and turned the corner.

Several young men and women were working at the desks. From time to time they glanced up at Carter. But then they turned back to their work. This apparently was a thriving operation.

Katy Shwartz was back a minute or so later. "You can go right in, Mr. Carter," she said, pointing back the way she had come.

"Thank you, Katy," he said, smiling.

"I don't suppose you'll be staying for supper . . . maybe overnight?"

"I don't think so. But at any other time I'd be tempted. Believe me."

"Yeah?" she said. "Back there. He's waiting for you." She turned and went back outside.

Carter went down the corridor, knocked at the single door around the corner, and went inside.

Peri Sharon was a man in his fifties. Carter had seen several photographs of him in the AXE brief, but none of them had been taken after his encounter with Yamun, so Carter was totally unprepared for what the man had become.

Sharon sat propped up in an elaborate wheelchair, an electrical control bar to the left of his chin so that he could move himself around. One of his legs was missing to the hip, the other to the knee. His right arm was mostly gone, and his left hung nearly useless at his side. His face had been shattered by the bomb blast that had nearly killed him. Most of his nose was gone, he had no hair on his head, and much of the skin on his face and on the right side of his head was puckered and shiny where he had been horribly burned.

He smiled, his lower lip intact, his upper lip merely a thin pencil line of flesh.

"Katy says you are a visitor from Washington, D.C., Mr. Nick Carter."

"Yes, sir," Carter said, not quite sure what else he should be doing by way of greeting.

"Have a seat, have a seat," Sharon said. He hit the control bar with his chin, and the wheelchair moved in closer to his desk.

As Carter was sitting down, Sharon had grabbed a pointer with his teeth, and with it he keyed his intercom.

"Bring us a couple of bottles of beer. My guest looks thirsty," he said. Sharon replaced the pointer. "So, Mr. Carter, I suspect you've come to ask me something."

"About Abd-el Yamun," Carter said. He took out his cigarettes. "Do you mind?" he asked.

"Not if you light me one."

Carter did, reached over, and placed the cigarette between Sharon's lips. The Israeli inhaled appreciatively.

"Very nice," he said.

A young man came in a moment later with a couple of bottles of beer. One of them had a long straw in it. He looked at Sharon's cigarette disapprovingly but said nothing. He handed Carter his beer, then set Sharon's in a special wire rack to the left of his mouth. All Sharon had to do was turn his head to drink.

The young man left. Sharon managed easily to drink his beer from the straw and yet hold the cigarette in his mouth.

"I won't ask you if you're with the CIA, because I suspect

you wouldn't tell me one way or the other. But I'd like to know if you're armed at the moment.''

Carter nodded.

"With what?'' Sharon asked sharply, his eyes narrowing.

Carter showed him his Luger and the stiletto.

Sharon grinned. "The blade is nice. From the looks of you, you know how to use it.''

"There's been an occasion or two.''

Sharon laughed out loud. Choking. Carter half rose out of his chair, but Sharon nodded him away.

"I'm all right, dammit,'' he snapped, coughing. "I'm not supposed to drink or smoke. I'll be out of it within a few minutes. Alcohol and nicotine don't mix with all the crap they've been pumping into me to keep me alive. So if you want to know something about Yamun, ask me now. No futzing around.''

Carter decided he liked the man a lot. He had probably been one hell of a Mossad agent before the bomb had cut his career short.

"Yamun is on his way out.''

"I know that. Lapides from Aman was here stroking me.''

Carter had to grin. "How the hell do you know I'm not the opposition?''

"What do you think I am, stupid? The moment you got off the plane in Tel Aviv I knew about you. They say you're CIA, but your background is a little fuzzy. You probably work for the State Department. Always thought those bastards had a special secret service. Too many unanswered questions . . .''

"I want to get to him.''

Sharon laughed again. "You look tough, and I hope you're not stupid. Everyone wants to get to Yamun.''

"I mean, I want him alone.''

"To kill him or bring him back for trial?''

Carter's eyes went flinty.

Sharon shook his head. "No . . . you're not the type who

would bring someone like that back for trial. Too many variables." He sat forward. "Lapides is pissing in his pants over this. He's so frightened of Yamun he can't move. They all are. They want Yamun back here in chains like a big monkey in a zoo. Like King Kong."

"I won't be bringing him back to Israel."

"No," Sharon said. "And we really don't want him back here. There's too much hurt thinking about the Olympics without bringing it all back." Sharon blinked and focused on Carter. "You're a goy, so you think all Jews are guilt-ridden. But listen to me, Carter. You don't really know just how true that is. You know, there are even Jews who are guilty about Hitler and the Holocaust." Sharon laughed bitterly. "Sure. They feel guilty because they let it happen. They didn't do enough to stop it. Can you imagine that?"

"Can you help me?" Carter asked carefully.

Sharon looked closely at him. "You've got that hard look about you, Carter. Just like Yamun." He shuddered. "You're brothers, I think. Just on different sides of the fence."

Carter said nothing. It didn't matter what Sharon said to him, how harshly he baited him. What mattered was information.

"Beirut. He has a sister there. No one knows it. No one suspects. It's his big secret."

There was nothing about any sister in Yamun's file. Nothing at all. He had a mother and father, both dead in Lebanon, and a brother who had been killed while fighting with the PLO out of Syria five years ago. But there was nothing about a sister.

"It's true. She is his younger sister. Miriam Yamun. She still lives in Beirut."

"How do you know about her?" Carter asked.

"She was my prize, Carter," Sharon said. His words were beginning to slur. "I knew about her. I learned about her when I was an undercover agent in Beirut. Four lousy years. But I found out about her." Sharon looked away. "She was beautiful, I'm telling you. Beautiful.''

"Is she still there?"

"Oh, yes," Sharon said, still looking away. "He comes to visit her before each mission. Stays a few days. Maybe a week, whatever.''

"And you found out about this somehow?"

Sharon looked at Carter. He nodded. "I tortured a man to death for the information. I killed his father in front of his eyes. And then I threatened to rape and kill his mother unless he told me. He talked.''

"Wouldn't they have informed Yamun?"

Sharon shook his head. "I killed them all, afterward." His eyes were very bright. "I wanted Yamun! Nothing would stand in my way!''

Carter suddenly understood an important fact of Sharon's past. "Who was on the Olympic team in Munich that year? Your brother?"

"Two brothers," Sharon said, tears coming to his eyes. "I figured anything was fair. I would get the son of a bitch. But it was a setup from the beginning. From day one. He knew I was there. And she knew what I had come for.''

"You saw her? You met with her?"

"I was going to get close to her, and then when he showed up, I was going to blow both of them away.''

Carter now understood one final fact of Sharon's life.

"Where does she live?"

He gave Carter an address just off the once fashionable Ras Hamara Street, downtown. "She is a fashion model. Beautiful.''

"And you fell in love with her?"

Sharon pursed his disfigured lips. "I wasn't bad-looking in those days . . .''

Carter got up. He reached over and took the nearly finished cigarette from Sharon's lips and ground it out in an ashtray on the desk. "Thanks," he said. But Sharon did not hear him.

THREE

Esterman was waiting for him when he got back to the Sheraton. The hotel had given him a key, and the CIA liaison man was sitting, propped up on the bed, drinking a scotch and water.

This was the second time something like this had happened to Carter on this assignment so far. He was beginning to get disturbed about it, and he told Esterman that.

"Take it easy, Carter, I'm not the opposition," Esterman said, swinging his legs off the bed and getting up.

"What are you doing here?"

"You wanted to be briefed? You're going to be briefed."

"When?"

"Now. At Aman headquarters. David Lapides has something he wants to say to you personally. Aharon Levi—he's a Mossad type—will be there as well."

Carter stared at the man for a moment. Esterman was *not* the opposition; he was nothing more than a jerk.

"Let me get cleaned up . . ."

"They're waiting for you now," Esterman said. "I've been here an hour. Where have you been?"

"Let's go, then," Carter said, ignoring the question. He turned back to the door.

"Are you armed?"

"Yes."

"You won't get through the metal detectors, and they'll kick your ass out of Israel," Esterman said smugly.

Carter turned to him. "You're the CIA liaison to the Israeli secret services. Are you telling me you run around Tel Aviv and you're not armed? Every goddamned Arab kid is toting a packet of plastique, and you're not armed?"

"I'm a liaison man here—"

"I'm not," Carter snapped.

"Just what are you?"

"Beyond the fact that I am an American here representing American interests, what I am or who I am is none of your goddamned business."

Esterman said nothing.

"Go downstairs and wait for me out front. I'll be right down."

"We're late already."

"Get the hell out of here," Carter growled. He pulled open the door and stepped aside. Esterman hurried out.

Carter pulled off his clothes and weapons, took a long cool shower, then repacked his weapons in the cassette recorder and set the machine out in the open on the dresser where it would be so obvious, chances would be no one would bother with it. He made one phone call.

When he was dressed he went downstairs. Esterman was waiting in his car. They drove into town to a building marked MILITARY ACQUISITIONS SECTION and parked around back. Esterman led the way inside, and they were both checked with a security scanner before being escorted upstairs.

David Lapides and Aharon Levi were waiting in Lapides's office.

Esterman made the introductions, and afterward they all sat down.

"Welcome to Israel, Mr. Carter," Lapides began. "Can you fill me in as to exactly why you are here?"

"Yamun is on the loose, and I'm here to help out."

"We neither need nor want your help."

Carter grinned. "I'm here in any event. If you want to order me out of your country, you may, but it will not be necessary."

"No?" Levi said.

"I'm leaving this evening. The Nicosia flight."

Lapides sat forward so fast he almost fell off his chair. "What information do you have about Yamun? Is he on Cyprus?"

Carter shook his head. "I honestly don't know."

Lapides's eyes narrowed. "Goddamn you, I am not going to play games here. If you have any information regarding any aspect of this investigation—and I do mean *any* aspect —I want that information this instant, or else I'll throw your ass in jail."

Carter took out a cigarette and lit it, taking his time. "I'm not Esterman. I've come here to help. My understanding is that you do not want my help, so I'm leaving."

"Why not to Paris, or direct to Washington? What's in Nicosia?"

Carter smiled. "My girlfriend."

Lapides slammed his fist on the desk top. But Carter just shook his head.

"All joking aside, Mr. Lapides, I did come to Israel to help. And I came here this afternoon specifically for my briefing. If you are not interested, then I'll contact my embassy and they can work it out. Meanwhile, with or without your briefing I am leaving Israel this evening. But I may be back."

Lapides and Levi looked at each other.

"Where were you this afternoon, Mr. Carter?" Levi asked.

"I went for a drive in the countryside. Lovely."

Lapides was on the verge of exploding.

"We'll find out sooner or later," Levi said.

Carter shrugged.

"You have no authorization to conduct any investigation on Israeli soil."

"I understand that. So I'm leaving."

Lapides got to his feet. "I don't think so," he said.
Carter looked up at him.

"Not until you answer our questions."

"Am I under arrest?" Carter asked calmly.

"Yes, you are," the Aman chief replied tightly.

"And Esterman? Is he under arrest as well?"

This surprised Lapides. He shook his head. "Why, no. Of
course not. He's done nothing."

"Fine," Carter said. He turned to the CIA liaison. "I want
you to leave now. Get over to our embassy and tell them what
is happening here. They can call Washington. But they'll
have to hurry. I have a flight to catch in less than three
hours."

"Wait a moment!" Lapides shouted. Esterman was stunned.

"Is Burt free to go?" Carter asked sharply.

"Yes, but . . ."

"Get the hell out of here, now!" Carter snapped. "There
isn't much time."

Esterman jumped up.

"I said, wait a minute," Lapides repeated sternly.

Carter shook his head. "I'm either under arrest, in which
case I want Esterman to run my errand, or I'm not, in which
case I'll return to my hotel."

"You won't answer our questions?" Levi, who was much
calmer than Lapides, asked.

"No," Carter said.

"Why?"

"I was sent here to help. You don't want my help. I'm
going."

"There's more to it than that," Levi insisted.

"Yes, there is. You're not going to share your work with
me, and neither will I with you. Now, what's it to be?"

Lapides stared at him for a long time. He finally waved
him toward the door. "Get the hell out of here, Carter, before
I do have you thrown in a cell."

Carter got to his feet.

"If you get in our way, if you should happen to get in the line of fire between us and Yamun, it will not only be the mad dog you will have to worry about."

"It's comforting to know you're friends," Carter said. He turned and left the office, Esterman right behind him.

"I don't know what the hell *that* was all about, but I can assure you every bit of it will be in my report to Washington," the CIA liaison complained.

Carter ignored him until they were back outside in their car. "Get me back to my hotel."

Esterman looked at him. "I've got a mind to arrest you myself for interfering in Israeli government business."

Carter turned narrowed eyes to him. "My hotel, Burt. Now."

Esterman jumped. "Ah . . . yes . . ." he said, not exactly sure if even those two words were too much.

They drove back to the Sheraton without another word. Carter got out in front of the hotel, and without looking back, he went inside. A moment or two later a very confused Esterman went back to his office to figure out exactly what he should do next.

Up in his room Carter repacked his bags, then telephoned the desk to get his bill ready.

Esterman would cause no further trouble, Carter figured. The man might try to make some waves through the embassy to Washington, but Hawk would see to it that he was stepped on quietly.

Either Aman or the Mossad—or perhaps both Israeli secret services—would put someone onto Carter's trail. He was certain of at least that much. It made perfect sense. He had seen the look that passed between Lapides and Levi back at the Aman office. Rather than have him arrested, they figured they'd learn more if they let him go and followed him.

Let them, Carter thought, leaving his hotel room. He would go to Beirut and try to find Miriam Yamun. Her face would mean nothing to the Israelis, according to Peri Sharon. And if by chance Yamun was there, Carter was going to kill him immediately, no questions asked. By the time his Israeli tail or tails had a chance to react, it would be all over.

There would be some surprised people here in Tel Aviv. Some very surprised people.

Carter paid his bill and outside got a cab for Lod Airport. As he settled back for the ride, another thought struck him.

Yamun had always been a step or two ahead of the Mossad and Aman. Was it possible, he asked himself, that the man had a link with the Israeli secret services? If he had someone within either organization to tell him when a move was being made against him, he'd never be caught.

He'd know now that Carter was on his way to Nicosia. He'd be able to put two and two together and figure that Carter would be coming to Beirut.

But would the terrorist take the information one step further? Would he understand that somehow Carter had found out about his sister and was going after her?

All that was merely speculation, of course. But it was that kind of speculation that had kept Carter alive for so long.

Yamun was a tough opponent. With a pipeline into the Israeli secret services, he would be awesome.

The Syrian national airline was running several flights a day from Nicosia into the Beirut airport whenever a lull came in the fighting and the airport was temporarily opened. The flights served international customers, many of them Jewish businessmen from France and from the U.S. who could not get into Beirut in any other way.

Carter had to wait for more than an hour at the Nicosia airport before he and the other passengers were allowed to board the DC-10 for the forty-minute flight across.

There were rumors that the Beirut airport was once again under attack, and flights were being held up.

Even at night from the air it was evident, coming in, that Beirut was a city that had been under siege for a long time.

Carter had been in the city before the troubles started, and off and on over the past years as its troubles progressed. It always saddened him to see such a once great city going to pieces. At one time Beirut, with its fashionable avenues, had been considered the Paris of the Middle East. That was no longer true.

They touched down a little after 8:30 P.M. and were held up at the far end of the taxiway for fifteen minutes before they finally moved to the terminal.

Carter took a cab into town. The driver, a young Lebanese, was extremely nervous. There had been a clash along this road just a couple of hours earlier. This was a very unhealthy place to be. An Israeli Uzi submachine gun lay on the seat next to the young man. From time to time he would look down at it, and then reach out and touch the wire stock, just to reassure himself.

Carter lit a cigarette and passed the pack up to the driver, who gratefully took one.

"Big trouble here tonight?" Carter asked.

"Yes, sir. Plenty big trouble tonight. And every night. It will never end, you know."

Carter reached into his bag and by feel withdrew his weapons from his cassette recorder.

"The Hilton is still okay," the driver was saying. "All the journalists and foreign businessmen stay there. Plenty good drinks."

"I'm leaving in the morning."

"You getting out plenty quick. You going to do business tonight? Here in the city?"

"Yes," Carter said, shoving his Luger into his shoulder holster.

"At the hotel?"

"No. I have to meet with someone. Maybe you can help."

The driver was startled. He looked at Carter's image in the rearview mirror. "What? You a spy, maybe?"

Carter threw back his head and laughed out loud. "A spy? Do I look like a spy? That's rich. I mean that's really rich."

The driver kept glancing up at the mirror.

"But I'll need help making my meeting," Carter said. He pulled out a couple of hundred dollars in American tens and twenties. He held them up.

The driver looked at the money. "Everything in Beirut is dangerous these days," he said to himself, licking his lips. He started to reach over his shoulder for the money but then stopped. "What is it? What do I have to do?"

Carter's right hand went into his jacket, his fingers curling around the butt of his Luger while he still held the wad of money over the seat with his left. He gave the man an address. "There is a woman I must see there."

The driver shrugged nervously. "So, big deal. So what?"

"She doesn't know I'm coming. She mustn't know I'm coming."

"She's got a husband? Maybe a crazy, jealous boyfriend?"

"A brother who doesn't like me."

"So . . . a brother," the driver said. "So maybe you want to find him and kill him?"

"Maybe," Carter said.

The driver hesitated only a moment longer, then he reached back for the money and stuffed it in his jacket pocket. "So let's go," he said. "What the hell do I care anyway?"

There was a fair amount of traffic into the city because of the flight from Nicosia, and the young driver kept looking nervously in his rearview mirror.

Closer into the shattered downtown area, along Ras Hamara Street, there were a lot of army trucks and jeeps, some of them Italian equipment, some French, but mostly U.S. vehicles that had been left over from the peacekeeping forces that had been here.

On many corners machine gun emplacements had been set up behind sandbag barriers. Not very effective against a concentrated sniper attack from the upper floors of tall apartment buildings nearby.

Beirut reminded Carter of Saigon during that city's last

days. Residents were attempting to keep some semblance of normalcy, but everyone had a siege mentality. Everyone knew that an attack could come at any moment from any quarter.

It was as if a terrible electrical current constantly flowed through the atmosphere, affecting everything and everyone.

"We go this way now," the driver said, turning off the main boulevard. The Hilton was in sight a couple of blocks away.

Within a hundred yards of the wide avenue, they came to a section of narrow, debris-choked streets where it became very difficult to maneuver the cab, let alone continue. Carter had visions of coming into a box canyon. It would not take much for them to be cut off from any chance of escape.

Carter sat forward. The driver had slowed down, and they were barely crawling along.

"This is bad back here," the driver said. He kept looking up toward the roof lines.

"How far do we have to go?"

"Next block."

"Stop here. I'll go the rest of the way on foot."

The driver stopped and looked back at Carter. "I don't think I want to stay here very long. Especially if you're going to make trouble."

There was no one in sight. No traffic. No pedestrians. It was as if they had come into a deserted city. The battle was coming, and everyone had retreated.

The Hilton was a half-dozen blocks back to the west. Not an impossible distance on foot. But everything was changed in the city since Carter had last been there. With all the damaged buildings and rubble-filled streets, it was difficult to recognize anything.

Carter checked Wilhelmina to make sure a shell was in the chamber, then he patted the young driver on the shoulder.

"I'm getting out here. Take my bags over to the Hilton and check me in. The name is Carter. Tell them I'll be there later tonight."

"Are you crazy?" the driver protested, wide-eyed. "You'll never get out of here alive."

"That's my worry . . ." Carter started to say, when the driver glanced up at the rearview mirror and stiffened.

"Uh-oh."

Carter turned around to look out the rear window. A cab was making a turn on the narrow street a block behind him. It took off in a big hurry back toward Ras Hamara.

"Someone got out," the driver said.

"One, two? How many?"

"Just one. They went into one of the buildings."

Carter studied the area for several moments, but there was no movement other than the retreating lights of the cab, which finally disappeared around a corner.

It could be nothing, he thought. But it was damned coincidental that someone was back there. Was someone following him? Yamun, perhaps? It made his skin crawl.

"Get my things back to the hotel," Carter said, and he got out of the cab.

"Hey . . ." the driver shouted, but Carter headed down the street, keeping well within the deeper shadows to one side.

He had gone less than fifty yards when the cab turned around and headed back toward Ras Hamara. Within a few moments Carter was alone, silence descending on the narrow street.

For a minute or so he remained where he was, watching the buildings behind him. Waiting for a sign, any movement, that would tell him he had indeed been followed. But there was nothing, and after a while he turned and continued toward the address that Peri Sharon had given him.

The area smelled of plaster dust from downed buildings, of open sewers, and of natural gas. But he could also smell something cooking, the odors faint and not unpleasant on the very light breeze that penetrated this far into the city.

There were people living here. He could feel their presence, just as he could feel that he was being watched, that his every movement was being followed.

If Yamun was back there, following him, this could very well be a trap.

He paused again at the intersection of a very narrow alley. Miram Yamun's building was just across the way. He could see the number plainly marked over the doorway of the small shop Sharon had described. He looked up. Her apartment was on the second floor. There were no lights in the windows.

A trap? he wondered. Or had she moved? It had been many years since Sharon had been here. Was his information still accurate?

There was no movement in the alley. The burned-out hulk of an old car lay at an angle farther up the alley. Something had been written in white paint on its doors, but Carter couldn't make it out from where he stood.

He clicked Wilhelmina's safety off and stepped across the alley at the same moment two people burst out of the shop door. He got the impression that both were dressed in battle fatigues as he rolled left toward a pile of rubble, snapping off two quick shots as he fell.

The narrow street exploded with gunfire, the bullets whining off the pavement just behind Carter, then exploding in the pile of rubble as he gained its relative safety.

Carter popped up and snapped off a third shot at one of the figures in battle fatigues, who fell to the ground, then he pulled his head down as automatic fire raked the pile of bricks.

A motorcycle started up in the alley, and Carter rolled right, keeping low around the far edge of the pile. He managed to get off one shot at the retreating figure on the bike, but it went wide, and the bike was gone.

More automatic fire ricocheted off the pavement inches from Carter's head as he rolled back. In a split second he saw the second man in battle fatigues leaping for the protection of the shop door. Carter fired two quick shots, the first exploding the back of the man's head, the second slamming him through the window, glass and blood spraying everywhere.

A silence fell over the street as Carter ducked back and hurriedly changed clips in his Luger. A moment or two later he looked up over the top of the rubble heap.

Both of his assailants were dead. There was no other movement on the street.

Hesitating only a moment or so longer, Carter scooted out from behind the pile and, running in a zigzag pattern, made it across the street to the corner of the doorway into the shop.

There was no one there. No one in the street or the alley. And no one within the shop.

He glanced down at the body half in and half out of the window, and his stomach flopped. Flowing from either side of the terrible head wound was long, dark hair. It was a woman.

"Christ," he said. "Oh, Christ." He reached in and carefully turned the body over, and looked at what in life had been the face of a beautiful woman.

Miram Yamun.

Carter looked around the corner and down the alley. Yamun had been there. It had been he who had left on the motorcycle, leaving his sister and the other one to cover his trail.

FOUR

Carter took the morning flight back to Nicosia where he had to wait an hour and a half for the next El Al flight to Tel Aviv. He kept seeing Miram Yamun's face in death, and he could not put out of his mind what she must have looked like in life. He could well understand why Peri Sharon had fallen in love with her.

He had gone upstairs and quickly and efficiently searched her apartment, finding absolutely nothing connecting her to her brother. But he hadn't expected anything different.

For a half hour he had hung around in the shadows across the street, hoping against hope that Yamun might return to see how his sister and the man had made out.

Yamun never returned, of course. Carter hadn't really expected that either. Finally he had to leave the neighborhood when sirens sounded in the distance. Even in a city as violent as Beirut had become, reports of shootings were investigated sooner or later.

He had had no trouble making his way to the Hilton, where his bags were waiting for him in his room. Neither did he have any problems leaving the city.

He waited now in a phone booth in the Nicosia airport for his call to Washington to go through. The connection was finally made and was answered on the first ring. It was Hawk's private number.

43

"Yes," came the old man's gruff voice over the transatlantic line.

"I'm in Nicosia. I've just left Beirut."

"Did you make contact?"

Quickly and succinctly Carter explained what had happened, leaving out nothing.

"They're not going to welcome you back with open arms in Tel Aviv," Hawk said, guessing what Carter's next move would be.

"Sharon helped us once; I think he'll help again."

"If he knows anything further."

"I think he does."

Hawk was silent for a moment. "They've made quite a stir. If you're going back, I want you in and out within twelve hours."

"Can do," Carter said. "Anything you can do from your end to hold them off?"

"I doubt it, but I'll speak with State," Hawk said. "But tread lightly. This is almost as big a thing to them as Eichmann was. They might shoot first and apologize later."

"Yes, sir."

"Good luck," Hawk said, and he hung up.

There was a hold on Carter's passport in Tel Aviv, and while he waited for the customs officer to finish his telephone call, he was certain that they'd hold him at the airport and make him take the next flight out. To anywhere.

But the customs officer came out of his office and with a pinched smile handed Carter his passport.

"Welcome to Tel Aviv, Mr. Carter. We hope you enjoy your stay," the officer said.

Surprised, Carter stepped out of the customs area, crossed the terminal to the Hertz counter, and rented a small Chevy for the day.

There was a lot of traffic on the main highway from Lod Airport, so he did not even bother looking for a tail until he had turned off to the north, away from Tel Aviv and directly up to Gan Har 'Evm kibbutz. Almost immediately he picked out the dark gray Opel behind him, and he relaxed. They were tailing him, which meant there would be no surprises. They wanted to find out what he was up to.

Carter figured Sharon was an old enough hand in the business to take care of himself, and yet he found he could not repay the man's help by simply leading a man and the Mossad to his doorstep. They might not do anything drastic to him, but they certainly would not look kindly on his actions.

A couple of miles farther, he cut back toward the west on one of the secondary highways that led directly into Tel Aviv and sped up. The Opel made the turn behind a couple of trucks a half mile back.

Carter sped up even more, passing two cars and a bus as the road curved, putting even more distance between himself and his tail.

He concentrated on his driving for the next fifteen minutes, going very fast, taking a lot of chances passing traffic, making it more and more difficult for the Opel to ever catch up.

Then he was within Tel Aviv, taking random turns from the main streets, finally ending up in a parking garage a couple of blocks from the Shalom Meir tower downtown.

He took a cab over to the Histadrut Building, then a bus across to the central railway station, where he rented a Ford Cortina.

Through all of that he made sure that no one was following him. It would take them the rest of the day to find his car and realize what he had done. Long before that, he figured, he'd be done with his business. Back in the city, he'd turn in the Ford, retrieve the other car from the parking garage, and get back out to the airport.

Customs would flag him, but he didn't think they'd stop him from leaving the country. At least he hoped they wouldn't, although with the temper Lapides had displayed it could be touchy.

Carter found his way out of the city, and once on the main

seacoast highway he no longer needed a map to return to the kibbutz.

He arrived back at Gan Har 'Evm in the early afternoon, the day every bit as hot as the day of his previous visit.

Several trucks containing what looked like electrical generators were parked just off the central square, and a dozen young people were busy unloading them.

Katy Shwartz was seated behind a desk in the administration building when he entered. She looked up and smiled.

"How about that," she said, rising. "You just couldn't bear to be without me."

Carter smiled. Everyone else in the office was grinning. "You say that to all the boys."

"Yup," she said. "I figure one of these days I might get lucky."

A young man laughed out loud. Katy turned to him and gave him a dirty look. He shut up.

"I'd like to see Mr. Sharon."

"I figured as much. But you're out of luck today."

"Is he gone?"

"No, just sick. He's at the dispensary."

"It's important I speak with him, Katy. It's very important."

Katy studied him for a moment. "Is it the Yamun thing again?"

Carter nodded.

She shook her head. "Look, I know he'll want to talk to you. It's his pet subject. But the last time you were here you damned near killed him. He's not allowed to have alcohol or tobacco. The mixture is deadly."

"I promise," Carter said. "All I need is about two minutes."

Katy hesitated a moment longer. But then she shrugged. "Come on," she said.

Carter followed her out of the administration building, across the central square, and into a small square building. It was the dispensary, but there was no sign announcing it, and there was no red cross painted anywhere.

He asked her about it.

"It would be the first place the Arabs would hit in a fire fight. We don't advertise the fact."

The doctor was gone, and the nurse objected to the visit. Nevertheless, she went into Sharon's room and told him that Nick Carter was there. They could hear Sharon bellow to allow him in.

"Just for a minute or two, Mr. Carter. Please. And no cigarettes!"

"Promise," Carter said. He went into the room. Sharon lay on a narrow hospital cot, his head propped up. He looked terrible. His skin had a blue tinge to it, and his eyes seemed filmy.

"Close the door and light me a cigarette," Sharon said.

Carter closed the door and came closer to the bed. "I had to promise I wouldn't."

"Hell," Sharon said. "I'm dying anyway. Can't you bend the rules?"

Carter shook his head. "I need to know more about Yamun. Where else besides Beirut does he operate from when he's breaking out?"

Sharon looked intently at Carter. "Did you go to Beirut? Have you seen . . . Miram?"

Carter took a deep breath and let it out slowly. "I was there. Yamun was there too."

"He was? My God, did you see him? Did you get a shot at him?"

"He was too fast. He got away."

"Damn. Damn," Sharon swore softly. "What about Miram?"

This was going to be very hard. Carter wished he could spare the man the grief his news would cause, but he was not going to lie to him. Not now.

"Miram and a man came out of the shop and fired at me. They were covering Yamun's escape."

"The bastard," Sharon said. But then understanding dawned in his eyes. "Miram . . . and the other . . ."

"They're both dead. I didn't know who they were. I had to kill them both."

"No doubt about identification?"

Carter described the woman to him. Sharon's eyes filled.

"It is her," he said.

Carter stood by the bed in silence for several moments, until finally Sharon looked up. "So, you're back for more information."

Carter nodded. "Yamun was at his sister's. He left. For where?"

"Paris," Sharon said matter-of-factly. "He has friends there. Try the Libyan embassy."

Paris! "Certainly he won't be staying at the embassy."

"No, the bastard's not that obvious. But he'll have runners. He'll need equipment. All his secondaries will be working out of the embassy. He'll be holed up somewhere nearby. But he'll have one hell of a bolt-hole, Carter. And he'll know about his sister. He'll know about you, and he won't be happy."

"What's his weakness?" Carter asked. "How do I get to him? How do I make him make a mistake?"

Sharon seemed to drift off for a moment or two. But then he focused. "His sister was his weakness. Now that she's gone . . . it could be his temper. He'll be very unpredictable now. Very dangerous." Sharon trailed off, and then he finally closed his eyes and slept.

Carter stared down at the pathetic figure for a moment or two longer, and then he left the room. The nurse stepped past him and went inside.

Katy Shwartz was waiting for him. "Did you get what you came for?"

Carter nodded. "He's one hell of a man."

"You don't have to tell me," she said. "We all know it here."

They went outside and crossed the square.

"So, you're off again?" she asked.

"Yes," Carter nodded. He kissed her on the cheek. "Thanks, Katy. Perhaps another time."

She grinned. "Sure," she said. "Get the hell out of here before I kidnap you."

Carter had no trouble on the return trip to Tel Aviv. He turned in the Cortina, took a cab over to the parking garage, paid the fee, and headed back out to the airport in the Chevy. The Opel was there, behind him within a half block.

He kept checking the rearview mirror as he made a couple of exploratory turns, only this time the Opel stuck close. He could just make out the driver but saw no one else in the car.

They had been damned good to find his parking space so quickly. But with the help of the entire Aman and Mossad, plus the military and civil police, it was possible.

He got back on the main highway, and sped up a little as he sat back and relaxed. He did not think they would stop him, although it was possible they'd want to ask him a few questions before they let him get aboard his flight.

He arrived at the airport twenty minutes later, turned in his car, and booked himself on the next El Al flight to Paris, which left at eight. It was only a little after six now.

His passport was checked at baggage inspection, and his suitcases were X-rayed, his weapons showing up only as parts of the complicated cassette recorder.

"Did you pack your own suitcases, sir?" the agent asked him.

"Yes, I did."

"Thank you, sir," the agent said, stamping his bags, then tagging them for Paris.

Carter turned to leave the baggage area, figuring he had plenty of time for a sandwich and a drink, when he ran headlong into two men dressed in dark business suits.

"Mr. Carter," one of them said. "Just this way, sir."

Without resisting, Carter allowed himself to be led around customs and into a small, plainly furnished office. Lapides from Aman was waiting inside. Alone.

The two men deposited Carter, then withdrew, locking the door.

"Have a seat, Mr. Carter," Lapides said. "It is still more than an hour before you have to board your plane. Your bags are safely checked, your ticket confirmed. We have plenty of time for a little chat."

Carter sat down and lit a cigarette. "It was pretty fast work for your people to find where I parked my car."

Lapides shrugged. "We have our means. But then it wasn't so good of us to have lost you in the first place."

"No, it wasn't."

Lapides nodded. He was obviously working very hard to keep himself in control. "Would you like to tell me where you went this afternoon?"

"For a drive in the country."

"In the country," Lapides repeated. "To see someone or something? Which?"

Carter studied the man for a moment or two. Lapides could cause a certain amount of trouble for him in Israel. At the least he could hold Carter until morning. Meanwhile Yamun was presumably on his way, or already in Paris. Whatever his plans were, they'd be that much closer to realization.

No, Carter thought, a delay would not be tolerable.

"Look, Lapides, I'll make a deal with you."

The Aman chief smiled. "Now, that's better. What sort of a deal do you have in mind?"

"I'll tell you about Beirut if you don't pry into where I went this afternoon."

Lapides's eyebrows knit. "What are you saying to me? This is my country. You waltz in here, wander around, make fools of my people, and then tell me it's none of my business?"

Carter shrugged. "I'm trying to cooperate with you," he said, leaning forward. "Let's say I have a friend in Israel who helped me. If I tell you her name, there might be trouble."

"She's a spy," Lapides snapped, picking up Carter's use of the feminine.

"No. A friend. She's done nothing illegal. I give you my word on it."

Lapides stared at him.

"I'm not the enemy."

"What about Beirut?"

"I found out that Yamun had a sister. Miram Yamun."

Lapides sat forward. "What . . . what?" he sputtered.

"I found out where she lived. And I also learned that Yamun often went to visit her."

"And you didn't tell us?" Lapides was furious.

"I wasn't sure of the information. And it wouldn't have made any difference."

"You went there? She was gone?"

"She was there, along with two men. One of whom was Yamun."

Lapides's fists were clenched in front of him, veins stood out on his neck, and his eyes were narrow. "Go on."

"I went there, and there was a fight. Yamun's sister and the other man were killed. Yamun escaped."

Lapides pounded his fists once on the table as he rose. Carter could see that he wanted to come across the desk with everything he had.

"I don't care how many of your people you could have brought in there. It wouldn't have made any difference. Yamun had been tipped off."

At first Carter wasn't sure if Lapides had heard him. But finally the Aman chief stood back.

"What did you say? What are you trying to tell me now?"

"Yamun has inside information, Lapides. It's the only way he's eluded capture for so long."

"What sort of inside information? Inside of what?"

"Aman or Mossad."

For a long time there was no noise in the small room other than the gentle sighing of the air conditioner. When Lapides spoke, his voice was very low and calm, but all the more menacing for it.

"I could kill you for that, Carter."

"You have had spies in your organizations before. We all have. Yamun has someone inside who feeds him information. He knew someone would be coming for him. He set up his own sister."

"You had the chance and you blew it."

"Right," Carter said.

"I want to know where you went this afternoon. Who is this mysterious informer of yours?"

"I told you about Beirut," Carter said, getting to his feet. "Deal's a deal."

Lapides pulled out a pistol, cocked the hammer, and pointed it directly at Carter's head. "You're not leaving this room alive unless you tell me what I want to know."

Carter turned back and leaned well over the desk, the muzzle of Lapides's pistol inches from his forehead.

"Go ahead and pull the trigger, Lapides. But before you do, consider something. You're crazy to get Yamun, because the man is nothing more than a killing machine. He's a maniac. A psychopath. He kills for the hell of it. Innocent boys and girls. Innocent people. It doesn't matter to him. You want him, and I understand that. But do you want him so badly that you're willing to become the same as he?"

Lapides said nothing.

"Yamun kills innocent people. You pull the trigger and you will have murdered someone not only innocent, but a person from a friendly country out to do the same thing as you. Stop the mad dog."

Still Lapides said nothing. The pistol never wavered.

Carter straightened up and left the office, letting the door slam shut behind him.

No one tried to stop him.

FIVE

It was past 11:00 P.M. when Carter arived at Charles de Gaulle Airport outside of Paris. The El Al plane landed at Aérogare 1, which was mostly for foreign airlines. He went through the green customs line because he had nothing to declare, and just made the 11:30 closing time for the foreign exchange counter where he changed a few hundred dollars into francs.

He had the cabby take him to the Lancaster Hotel just off the Champs-Elysées on the rue de Berri. It was a small, very quiet hotel. He had stayed there before. Someone had once told him that when American movie stars wanted to remain incognito in Paris, they stayed there. Carter had never seen one.

His room overlooked the pleasant courtyard. Once he was settled in, he ordered up a bottle of cognac and a couple of bottles of wine from a bellman who was sleepy until Carter flashed just the correct amount of a tip.

Almost certainly Lapides had not let him get away from Tel Aviv without placing a tail on him. Someone on the plane.

During the flight over he had tried to pick out who it might have been, without much luck. It could have been any one of a half-dozen or more people, including one very good-looking, dark-haired woman who was somewhat reminiscent in looks to Miram Yamun.

He had noticed no one in particular behind him at the airport, and it didn't seem as if he had been followed into the city.

Sooner or later, however, whoever was after him would be showing up at the hotel. Just in case he was meeting with someone.

Carter took a long, leisurely shower, and he was unpacking his weapons when someone knocked at his door. He flipped the coverlet over the cassette recorder and opened the door.

The bellman bustled in, set up the wine and cognac on a stand near the window, and then left once he was tipped.

Carter poured himself a cognac, lit a cigarette, and glanced out the window. There was a movement in the shadows below, but then it was gone, and he wasn't sure he had seen anything.

He finished unpacking his weapons and loaded his Luger, then flipped off the lights. He moved a chair over near the window and sat down with his feet up to wait for the dawn.

He had a clear shot from the window as well as toward the door.

It could have been nothing below. Or it could have been his Israeli tail. Or, considering the possibility there was a leak in the Israeli secret service, it could have been Yamun himself, although he doubted it. Yamun was on his way out to do something. Later, after he finished whatever it was he had planned, he would certainly be back for the man who had killed his sister. Carter wanted to get to him before that.

It was a very long night. The door was locked and chained, and there was no way up from the courtyard, so Carter allowed himself the luxury of dozing on and off through the early morning hours.

At first light he rose, took another shower, shaved, and then got dressed. He would go and see an old friend of his who worked for the SDECE, the French secret service. If anyone in France knew Yamun's whereabouts, or his old haunts, it would be Pierre Belmont, who was a special investigator with DS6, that part of the service that dealt with foreign nationals on French soil.

Several times in the past he and Carter had worked together, sometimes officially, and other times not quite so officially.

Belmont had been in the business for a very long time, and he held no illusions about his country or anyone else's. He had spent a few years in Washington, D.C., as liaison to the CIA, for whom he had always been convinced Carter worked.

He would almost certainly be willing to help now. But first Carter wanted to neutralize his Israeli tail. He did not want to lead Lapides to Belmont.

When he was ready, Carter left the hotel and took a cab over to St.-Germain-des-Prés on the Left Bank.

It was early, but already the tourists, pseudo-intellectuals, and the well-to-do dropouts who still considered themselves students were out and about.

He walked to a small café he knew near the Deux Magots and ordered coffee and croissants. He sat outside, and when his breakfast came he had the waiter cross the street and get the Paris edition of the *Herald-Tribune* for him from the kiosk.

The morning was pleasant, although Carter resented being held up this way because of the Israelis. He could understand, though, why they wanted the first shot at Yamun. If their positions were reversed, he knew he'd feel the same.

As he read the newspaper he kept watching for signs that he was being watched. Across the narrow avenue were several shops, including one that sold vegetables and another that sold meat. At the corner was a bakery, and across the street was another café. At each place people were already milling around. Each was perfect for a watcher to position himself.

Sooner or later they would betray themselves. They would

be caught staring. They would be caught remaining too long in one spot. Or they would emerge from one of the stores, having spent a long time without purchasing much of anything. All were giveaways.

Carter ordered a second pot of coffee when he was halfway through the paper. So far he had spotted nothing, and he was seriously considering giving up this spot.

If the tail was there, he was very good. Carter had not spotted anyone who qualified. Nor had the same car passed more than once. There were no cars or vans parked at a nearby vantage point, and he couldn't see anyone in any of the nearby windows.

The waiter came with his fresh coffee and Carter turned around to thank him, when he spotted the dark-haired beauty from the airplane. She was seated at one of the other sidewalk tables.

He glanced from where she sat to the corner. She had followed him here, realized what he was doing, and walked the opposite way around the block, coming to the café from behind, while Carter was busy watching the shops across the street.

He had to smile. She was pretty sharp.

She was reading a fashion magazine and drinking coffee. Carter got up and came across to her table. She looked up.

"Good morning," Carter said. "May I join you?"

"Who are you?" she asked in English with a poor imitation of a French accent.

"The question is, who are you?" Carter said, smiling. "Lapides sent you. I saw you on the plane. Was it you in the courtyard of the Lancaster last night?"

"I don't know what you are talking about, *monsieur*," she said, again in badly accented English.

"You have not done your homework, my little butterfly," Carter spat in rapid-fire French. "If you had, you would know I am fluent in French. Well?"

She looked at him for a moment or so, and then she went for her purse beside her.

Carter reached across the table, grabbed her wrist with his left hand, and scooped up the purse with his right. Before she could do anything, he sat down across from her, opened the purse, and extracted her passport. There was a small Beretta automatic in an inside pocket.

"What do you think . . ." She started to protest, but he gave her back her purse.

"If you pull out your gun and shoot me, it will be very hard to explain to the French police," Carter said in English. He opened her passport. It was Israeli and identified her as Anita Gabrud. Tel Aviv.

He looked up. Her hand was in her purse. She did not look happy; her nostrils were flared and her lips pursed. He handed her passport back.

"We're after the same thing here," Carter said.

"I don't know what you're talking about," she said. She put her passport back into her purse.

"Yamun."

Her eyes lit up. An instant later she realized she had betrayed herself by her own reaction.

Carter smiled and sat back. He motioned for his waiter and requested that his coffee be brought over. When they were alone again Carter lit a cigarette after offering her one. She declined.

"I think he may be here in Paris, or very nearby," he said.

"How do you know that?" she asked cautiously.

"The same way I knew he might be in Beirut. I got a shot at him there."

"But missed."

"Yes, but missed. He is very good. And he knew I was coming for him."

Anita nodded. She closed her purse and started to rise, but Carter motioned her back.

"Before you leave there is something you must understand."

She looked at him, then sat back.

"He knew I would be coming to Beirut—just as he knows I

am here—because someone told him.''

"How?" she asked.

"Someone within Aman or the Mossad told him.''

Her jaw tightened, and her eyes turned flinty. "I could kill you for that." Her words echoed Lapides's.

"Yes. But it's true nevertheless. So if you go back and tell them I am here on Yamun's trail, he will have another bit of ammunition to use against me. But you will not, because you will not catch up with me again.''

A faint flicker of a smile crossed her lips.

"And if you do stumble across me, I will probably kill you.''

"What do you want, Carter?"

"Yamun."

"He's ours!''

"It's been a long time since Munich. Have you caught up with him yet?''

"What makes you think you can do any better?''

"I don't know," Carter admitted. "But I'll do the job—or at least try—with or without your help." He finished his coffee and put down a couple of bills.

"What do you mean, with or without my help?''

"Exactly that," Carter said.

"Then you would accept my help?" she asked.

"Yes. But you would have to be on your own. The moment I thought you were reporting back, I would dump you.''

"I can't promise you that," she said in irritation.

"Fine," Carter said, shrugging. He got up and left the restaurant.

She came after him. "Wait a minute," she said.

Carter stopped.

"You want to kill him, don't you?" she said.

He nodded.

"My orders are to bring him back for trial.''

"It'll never happen. He won't allow it.''

"Those are my orders.''

"You'll get yourself killed."

"I said those were my orders. I didn't say that's what I'd do," she said. She smiled.

Carter grinned. "And you want me to believe you?"

"You've got that, or you can constantly be looking over your shoulder for me. And, Carter, I'll be there."

He sighed. "The name is Nick," he said, and he turned and headed up the street. She was right behind him.

They took a cab back across the Seine to within a block of his hotel. The Champs-Elysées was very busy by now.

"Yamun knows I'm here in Paris after him," Carter explained. "No doubt he knows my hotel, or will soon, and he'll be coming after me."

"Don't go back to your hotel," Anita said.

"I don't want to lose the chance that he'll make a mistake because of his sister."

Again Anita's jaw tightened. She had been told about Beirut.

Carter softened. "For what it's worth, I didn't know it was a woman, and she was shooting at me first."

"You want to stake out your hotel," she said.

"You'll do it. I have to see a friend here in Paris."

She shook her head. "I'm coming with you."

"No, you're not . . ." Carter started, but she held him off.

"No, you're right. Go ahead, I'll stake out your hotel."

Carter grinned. "Don't follow me. If you do, our deal is off."

"Will you tell me what you've come up with from your . . . friend?"

"Yes."

"I don't trust you, Carter," she said after a second. "But I don't want to fight you. I'll save it for Yamun."

"I'll be back in a couple of hours. As soon as I enter my hotel, come up," Carter said. He turned on his heel, hurried down the street, and hailed a cab a half block away.

He watched out the rear window as she headed up the street toward his hotel. He didn't trust her either.

Pierre Belmont's office was just off the rue St. Antoine, a couple of short blocks up from the Hôtel de Ville, in a section of buildings containing the offices of attorneys. Many of the SDECE's functions were conducted from satellite offices for reasons of economy as well as security. The French believed that a single bastion, such as the CIA's Langley building, could be breached. Dozens of smaller offices might be compromised, but only one at a time.

Carter dismissed his cab several blocks away and went the rest of the distance on foot, falling back several times, taking roundabouts, crossing the street, ducking into shops. But as far as he was able to tell, he was clean. Anita had either lost him, or she had been telling him the truth and was at the moment watching his hotel.

DS6 worked under the guise of a lawyer's office with a security guard stationed in the lobby.

"I'd like to speak with Monsieur Pierre Belmont," Carter said.

"Your name, *monsieur*?" the guard asked.

"Nick Carter."

"Have you an appointment?"

"*Non*."

The guard telephoned upstairs, announcing Carter's presence. Momentarily he looked up. "Would you care to go up? An escort will be sent."

"If Monsieur Belmont is there, please tell him to meet me for an early lunch at the usual place."

The guard's eyes narrowed, but he nodded and passed Carter's message along. "*Oui*," he said at last and hung up. "Your message has been received, *monsieur*."

"*Merci*," Carter said, and he left the building. It was still far too early for lunch at their usual place—the restaurant

Pierre-Traiteur on the rue de Richelieu just behind the Comédie Française—but Belmont would leave his office immediately, knowing that Carter would be behind him and would pick the rendezvous spot. It was standard tradecraft in the business.

Carter stepped across the street, and halfway down the block he stopped to light a cigarette and watch the front entrance to Belmont's building.

About five minutes later, Belmont, a tall, husky Frenchman with thick black hair and a very large, very Gallic nose, emerged, stopped to light a small cigar, and then turned left and headed in the same direction from which Carter had come.

Belmont spotted him almost immediately but gave no sign that he had, passing Carter's position and then turning down toward the river at the corner.

Carter recrossed the street and nonchalantly followed Belmont, keeping well behind the Frenchman. His senses were doing double duty; he was searching for a tail either ahead of or behind Belmont—in which case their meeting would be put off until sometime that evening—and at the same time he was keeping a continual watch on his own backside for any sign that Anita Gabrud had shown up.

But they were both clean.

Belmont worked his way past the Louvre, then at the Place de la Concorde, he doubled back, Carter out in front now.

A half hour later, both of them certain they were not being tailed, Belmont went down to the riverside walk and sat on a bench. Carter joined him five minutes later, after making one final check to make sure they were not being watched.

"We haven't done this for a long time, Nick," Belmont said without preamble.

"How are you, Pierre?"

"Just fine, my old friend. But this is extraordinary. What brings you to Paris?"

"Abd-el Yamun. Is the name familiar?"

"Ah, yes, the mad dog of the Olympics," Belmont said. He glanced up the river walk. "Are you after him? Is he here in Paris?"

"Perhaps."

"Do the Israelis know what you are up to?"

"Yes. And so does Yamun. I believe there is a leak in the Mossad or in Aman," Carter said. He quickly told Belmont everything that had occurred in Tel Aviv and in Beirut, leaving out only the identity of Peri Sharon.

"So you have been sent to kill him?"

"Yes."

"There will be much trouble if that happens on French soil, you know."

"Yes, I know, Pierre. It is why I have come to you."

"As a friend?"

"As a friend."

"How reliable do you believe your information is? Could Yamun not be in Paris?"

"I don't know. But now this is my only lead. We do know that he's coming out to do something."

"And it will not be pretty."

"No," Carter said. "In addition he will be gunning for me because of his sister."

Belmont shook his head. "A most unfortunate happening. You will have to be very careful, Nick. Very careful indeed."

"I need your help."

"Oh, yes, I know that. There will be activity around the Libyan embassy if he is here and ready to do his mischief. We will have to watch. It may provide us with a lead."

"He knows me, Pierre. He probably knows my face. If I get close to the embassy and word gets back to him, he will go deep."

"You want to take care of this once and for all?"

"Yes."

"Like Carlos. When will you go after him?"

"When I have orders to do so. This time it is Yamun I am after."

"And it is Carter *he* is after," Belmont said. "Yes, I will have their embassy placed under surveillance. We will make it loose. Routine. We do not want to arouse any suspicions. We want no passions other than *amour* here in Paris." He smiled wanly.

"If he is spotted, we can coordinate my actions with the SDECE."

"*Non*, Nick. If and when he is spotted, if it is at all feasible, we will turn our backs long enough for you to do your work and then leave."

"All right."

Belmont got to his feet. "Where are you staying?"

"The Lancaster on—"

"I know it. Is your Israeli watchdog there?"

"Yes."

"I see," Belmont said thoughtfully. "We will get word to you as soon as I have learned anything of value."

"Thank you, Pierre," Carter said.

A hard edge came to Belmont's voice. "This is the last favor I can do for you, Nick. After the last operation I came under much suspicion. I am up for promotion, and I mean to have it. The new position will let me afford a villa in the country. My wife wants this very much."

Carter was about to thank his old friend again, but Belmont turned on his heel and left.

SIX

Carter waited ten minutes after Belmont had gone, then he walked up past the Louvre to the rue de Rivoli and took a cab to St. Philippe's, just a block or so from the Lancaster.

He felt bad that his friend had put the condition on his help, but Carter knew that it would come sooner or later. In this business everyone used everyone else to the limit, and oftentimes beyond. Friendships were more fragile than life, it seemed, and certainly did not survive such handling.

There was a lot of traffic when he came around the corner, and he pulled up short a half block from his hotel.

A half-dozen police cars, their blue lights flashing, blocked the area directly in front of the hotel. An ambulance, its rear door open, was parked in the middle of the street, and a fair-sized crowd had gathered.

From the looks of things, whatever had happened had apparently just happened. The police were still pushing people back, and there was some sort of a commotion directly in front of the hotel entrance.

Carter scanned the crowd for any sign of Anita Gabrud, but he did not spot her.

He crossed the street to the same side as the hotel and headed toward the crowd.

A uniformed police officer stopped him within fifty yards of the front entrance. A body was being wheeled out of the hotel on the ambulance gurney and was loaded in the back.

"Please, you may not pass, *monsieur*," the policeman said in French.

"What's going on?" Carter asked in English.

"It is some trouble. It will be cleared in a moment," the policeman replied in halting English.

"But the Lancaster . . . it is my hotel," Carter said. "Will I be safe there?"

The policeman looked at him with new interest. "May I see some identification?"

"Of course," Carter said, and he produced his passport.

The policeman looked at it, then lifted a walkie-talkie to his lips. "Unit one, this is seven," he said in French.

"*Oui*," the tiny speaker hissed.

The policeman read off Carter's name and asked for confirmation that he was staying at the hotel. A moment later the walkie-talkie hissed again.

"*Moment.*"

The policeman looked at Carter.

"What does he look like?" the voice crackled.

The police officer relayed Carter's description.

"Yes, he is a guest here. You may allow him to pass."

The policeman handed Carter his passport. "You may procede, *monsieur*," he said.

"*Merci*," Carter said, and he pocketed his passport as he continued down the street to the hotel.

The ambulance pulled away, and the crowd began to disperse as Carter entered the lobby and approached the desk. There were police all over the place.

One of them stopped him, and he had to produce his passport again. The desk clerk and assistant manager were beside themselves. There were a lot of guests milling around, some of them demanding to be checked out, others demanding their rooms be changed.

"Where have you been in the past hour, *monsieur?*" the gendarme asked him.

"Walking along the river by the Louvre."

"You have witnesses?"

"No. I was alone."

"I see. What is your business in France, *monsieur?*"

Carter had been watching the activity at the desk. He focused on the gendarme now. "I am here on vacation. But this is terrible now. I wanted some peace and quiet."

"Here, at this hotel?"

Carter shrugged and grinned. "One can hope to see a movie star, perhaps."

The policeman smiled back and handed Carter his passport.

"What happened here?" Carter asked. "I saw a body."

"It was an unfortunate accident. A poor man fell down the elevator shaft."

"A workman?"

"Have a pleasant stay in Paris, *monsieur*. If you will excuse me?" The policeman touched his cap, then turned and went across the busy lobby.

At the desk Carter got his key and went up. The elevators were blocked off, so he had to use the stairs. His room was at the back on the third floor. He listened at the door before he unlocked it and started to go in.

There was a movement behind him, and he feinted to the left as he ducked low and reached for Wilhelmina, his hand stopping just within his jacket as he realized it was Anita Gabrud. She held her side and ran almost doubled over. She was hurt.

No one else was in the corridor as he helped her inside his room, then locked and chained his door. She collapsed on the floor.

Carter lifted her up and placed her on the bed. Her eyelids were fluttering, and she seemed to be in some pain. She was dressed in lightweight trousers, a silk blouse, and sandals.

Her clothing was torn and filthy. There was a long stain of thick black grease on her side, and the side of her face was scraped as if she had fallen against something very rough, such as concrete.

"What happened?" Carter asked.

At first there was no response.

"Anita," he said gently. "This is Nick Carter. What happened to you?"

Her eyes opened, and for an instant she tried to push away from him.

"It's all right," he said softly. "You're safe now."

Recognition came into her eyes, and she allowed herself to relax.

"What happened?" Carter asked again. He was sure she had had something to do with the commotion downstairs. "There are cops all over the place."

"Did they find him?"

"Find who?"

"The bastard who was here. He was a Libyan—I'd bet anything on it. He was here, trying to get into your room. I stopped him. There was a fight."

"They said he fell down the elevator shaft."

"They found him," she said, a faint smile crossing her lips. Her eyes fluttered again and she groaned. "My ribs. I fell."

"Where did you hide?"

Her eyes opened a moment longer. "In the old air shaft. I . . ." She swooned.

Carter felt her pulse. It was strong. He opened her blouse and pulled it aside. There was a long, ugly bruise on her side. He was sure she had cracked a couple of ribs. She would be sore for a few weeks, but he didn't think her injury would incapacitate her.

He went into the bathroom and ran some hot water in the tub, then called down to the bell captain and asked him to come up.

While he waited, he gently undressed Anita, tossing her clothes in a heap on the floor. She was long-legged and beautiful. Her breasts were lovely, her belly only slightly rounded.

He tossed a sheet over her casually, making sure that her thighs were well exposed and one breast was uncovered. It was going to have to look just right to be convincing. If the bell captain became suspicious and the police came up, their covers would be totally blown, and they would have to call it quits.

Pulling off his jacket, he tossed it aside, pulled off his tie, unbuttoned his shirt, and hid Wilhelmina.

A minute or so later the bell captain arrived, and Carter, out of breath and apparently frightened, let him in. When he spotted the girl on the bed his eyes went wide.

"You've got to help me! You've got to help me!" Carter babbled. "There're cops all over the place down there. If they find her like this . . . I'll go to jail!"

"What happened here?" the bell captain demanded.

"She'll be all right. I just need some bandages," Carter went on. He went over to the bed and flipped the sheet back, exposing her. The bell captain sucked in his breath.

"Who is she?"

"Doesn't matter. We had a fight, and I think I broke some ribs. She fainted. I just need some bandages."

The bell captain couldn't tear his eyes off her.

"If the cops find out . . . I'll lose everything," Carter said as he flipped the covers back over Anita, this time covering her entire body.

He pulled out several hundred francs and pressed them on the bell captain. "I need some bandages. But don't tell the cops. Whatever you do. Christ, I've got a wife and kids in Cleveland."

"Who is she?" the bell captain asked again.

"My secretary."

"She's not registered at this hotel?"

"Of course not," Carter said. "Now hurry! Please!"

"*Oui, monsieur,*" the bell captain said, and with one last glance at Anita, he left.

As soon as he was gone, Carter went into the bathroom and tested the bathwater, then he brought Anita in and gently lowered her into the tub. She groaned but didn't fully regain consciousness. He let her soak in the warm water for a few minutes, and then very gently cleaned her with soap and a washcloth.

He was just finishing when the bell captain returned with the bandages.

The man wanted to come in, but Carter wouldn't let him, and he left.

Carter pulled Anita out of the tub, dried her off, and brought her to the bed, where he bound up her cracked ribs. Her eyes fluttered and finally opened.

"What is it . . ." she started to say. "Where am I?"

"You're safe," Carter said. "How do you feel?"

She had half risen from the bed, but she lay back now and ran her fingers over the bandages at her side. "I fell from one elevator to the other," she said. Suddenly she realized that she was nude, and she tried to pull the covers over her.

Carter helped her despite her protestations, and when she was settled he smiled. She was angry.

"You took advantage of me," she accused.

"Not yet," Carter said, laughing. He poured them both a drink and brought hers to her. She took it gratefully.

"Thanks," she said. She lowered her eyes. "I waited until you returned. There were gendarmes everywhere."

"What happened?"

"There was a man here, at your room. We fought, and I killed him."

"In the corridor?"

Anita nodded. "I couldn't just leave his body lying around for someone to discover . . ."

"So you threw him down the elevator shaft."

She nodded. "It was not easy. And I fell in the process.

They found him almost immediately, and I had to hide."

"Evidently it wasn't Yamun," Carter said.

Something flashed in her eyes. "Obviously not," she said. "But he was an Arab. A Libyan . . . I'd bet my last sheckel on it."

"No identification?"

She shook her head, then finished her drink. She held out her glass for another. He poured her a second cognac.

He lit a cigarette, and she took it from him. He lit one for himself.

"You're going to have to run up to my hotel and get my things," she said.

"Is anyone watching it?"

"Not that I know of."

"I mean *your* people."

She looked at him, her nostrils flaring. She was a beautiful woman but a very typical sabra: extremely independent with a short fuse. "I came alone."

"Why don't I believe you?"

She smiled. "That's your problem."

"It's your problem at the moment," he corrected her. "Without me you won't get out of this hotel."

"Would you turn me over to the French police?"

"I'm after Yamun. Whatever it takes."

"Bastard," she said. "There is no one watching my hotel. I am alone there."

"But you didn't come to France alone."

"I have backup at our embassy here. But only if I call for it."

"Good enough," Carter said. "I'll wait a couple of hours for things to settle down, and then I'll go over. What hotel?"

"The California."

Carter had to laugh. It was barely a half block away.

"What about your friend?" Anita asked. "Did you learn anything?"

"It's possible Yamun is here in Paris. We'll know fairly soon."

Her eyes brightened. "How?"

"Whenever he comes to Paris he stays outside the city somewhere, of course. But there's always an increase in activity in and around the Libyan embassy. My friend will be watching. He'll let me know as soon as he finds out anything."

"He is with the police?"

Carter ignored her question. "Will you be able to move?"

"I think so," she said.

"Good." Carter went over to the window and looked down into the courtyard. There were several police and at least a dozen civilians, some of them almost certainly guests, down there. He noticed one man, a slight of build, somewhat dark man in one corner of the garden looking up. He spotted Carter, then slowly turned and walked away.

Carter looked back at Anita. She sensed something.

"What is it?" she asked.

"We may be having more company," he said, and he told her about the man. He got her purse from where he had tossed it with her clothes and gave it to her.

She opened it and took out her Beretta. She smoothly checked the action and the safety.

"They know we're here . . ." she started to say, but the telephone rang.

Carter picked it up. "Yes?"

It was Pierre Belmont. "I may have something for you," he said. "Can you talk?"

"Yes," Carter said.

"There was some trouble at your hotel. Was it related?"

"I think so."

The line was silent for a moment. "Do you wish some help?"

"Not that kind," Carter said. "What have you come up with?" Anita was looking at him.

"Something curious. But if it's our boy, he's changing his tactics."

Carter waited.

"The embassy was already under surveillance," Belmont said.

"By your people?"

"No, of course not. The Metro Police Organized Crime Division had a stakeout on it."

"Why?"

"It seems arms may be coming into France for the use of our underworld. Supplied by you-know-who."

"What's this got to do with our boy?" Carter asked. Yamun, when he used others, always used dedicated and well-trained terrorists. Using the French underworld would be a huge change in his strategy.

"They have a certain farmhouse spotted near Aubervilliers. It is just to the northwest of the city."

"I think I know it," Carter said. "South of St.-Denis."

"That is the place. They believe the head of the foreign connection is there now, negotiating with the underworld leaders."

"It does not sound like Yamun," Carter said, half thinking out loud.

"No, it does not. But he has gotten where he is because he never falls into a mold. It would be very dangerous for him."

Carter thought about that for a moment. "Has he actually been spotted?"

"No. But of course they are not looking specifically for him. They may very well have spotted him and not known it. The surveillance photographs are being brought over to me. I'll have them within a half hour, and then we may know something."

"Is the place still under surveillance?"

"Yes, it is."

"How do you want to work this?"

"This has all been worked out very carefully, so listen closely to what I have to say. I will pick you up at the Sacre Coeur in exactly two hours. On the side of the Place du

Tertre. From there we will drive directly to Aubervilliers. We will be observers. When we go in, you will make it your job to target our boy."

"And afterward?"

"Afterward nothing. If it *is* him, the newspapers will never know. He will remain an unidentified criminal shot and killed while attempting to smuggle weapons into France for illegal purposes."

"And I will melt into the background."

"Exactly."

"I'll be there."

"Alone."

Carter looked at Anita. She knew something was happening, and she seemed excited. "Right," he said. Belmont hung up.

Carter put the phone down and turned to Anita. She definitely knew something was going on.

"What is it?" she asked.

"They think they may have spotted him in a farmhouse just outside the city."

Her eyes were suddenly bright. "Where?" she asked. "And when do we get to him?"

Carter shook his head. "It's not quite that simple." Quickly he explained to her what the setup was, without naming Belmont and without disclosing the location of the farmhouse.

"Your friend knows that I've come along to watch you?" she asked cautiously.

"Yes, he does. But he told me we would do this alone. He and I. If you tag along, the deal is off."

"I don't care," Anita snapped. "I'm not letting you out of here without me." She shoved the covers back and got out of bed. She swayed for a moment, but then recovered her balance, grabbed her dirty, torn clothes, and headed for the bathroom.

"You wouldn't get past the lobby in that outfit," Carter said. She had a lovely body, and one hell of a derrière.

She turned back, holding her clothes up so that she was covered. "Then go get my things from my hotel."

"Only if you promise to remain here," Carter said evenly.

"I can't do that, Nick. Not and blow a chance to get at Yamun."

"If you follow me, there will be *no* chance, goddammit! Can't you understand that?"

Anita looked at him. Deliberately she lowered her clothes, then let them fall to the floor. She came a couple of steps closer. "Do you want me, Nick? You can have me now."

He smiled and nodded. "Yeah, I want you. But not like that."

"You son of a bitch . . ." she cried, and she charged, her fists upraised.

Carter reached up to ward off the expected blows, but she was a lot sharper, and certainly better trained, than he thought she was.

She had his left arm, and suddenly he was falling backward, slamming hard on the floor. A second later she had scrambled to the bed where she grabbed her Beretta and pointed it at him.

Carter slowly got up and stood facing her. She was in some pain—he could see it in her eyes—but she was excited. She was breathing rapidly, and her nipples were erect.

"You can shoot me if you'd like, but you'd never get out of France alive. They'd hang you!"

"I don't care."

Carter took a step closer. "I promised that we would work together, if you would cooperate. My sources will not help if you tag along. It's as simple as that."

"Stay back," she said.

"If Yamun is there and I manage to kill him, then our jobs will be done. You can go home. If he's not, or if he escapes, or if he kills me, you'll still be able to go after him." Carter took another step forward. He reached out and took the gun from her and laid it aside.

"You son of a bitch," she cried again, and she swung at

him. But this time Carter was ready.

He grabbed her wrists and shoved her back on the bed. She struggled for a moment or two, kicking and biting and trying to scratch, but then she was kissing him, her arms around his neck.

"Oh, hell," she cried.

She was an extraordinary woman. Carter found himself responding to her despite the fact that she was injured, despite the fact that she had threatened twice to kill him, and despite the fact that Belmont would be waiting to pick him up at the Sacré-Coeur in less than two hours.

He kissed her breasts, taking her nipples into his mouth, teasing them with his tongue and his teeth.

Her eyes were wide and bright. "This is insane," she said, shivering.

For a long moment Carter looked at her, and then shook his head. He started to back off.

"No," she said, reaching out for him. "No conditions. No commitments."

"You're hurt."

"Not that badly," she said, smiling. She sat up and began unbuttoning Carter's shirt.

She smelled very good, very feminine. Carter took her face in his hands and slowly, gently kissed her full, sensuous lips. Her tongue flicked out, brushing the end of his.

He caressed the soft skin of her back, following down the arch of her spine, his fingers brushing softly until he encountered the soft down just above her buttocks.

They parted. Her eyes were very bright, her nostrils flared and her lips moist.

Carter got up and slowly undressed. She watched his every movement, hungrily, as if she were a feral animal who would at any moment leap out of the bed and devour him where he stood.

There was a very great, unfulfilled need in her; he could feel it as a magnetism that seemed to fill the room with its urgency.

"Nicholas . . ." she cried softly. Her breasts were rising and falling. She reached out for him as he came into bed, her hands closing around his erection.

She mumbled something in Hebrew that he didn't quite catch, as he pushed her back on the bed, gently spread her legs, and began kissing her. He ran his tongue from the nipples of her breasts, down the cleft, along and around the soft roundness of her belly, finally brushing once, lightly across the moist lips of her vagina.

She shuddered, and moaned.

Carter gently rolled her over. She was limp, totally unresisting now, and he began kissing her ankles, working his way slowly up the backs of her legs, then to the small of her back, up to her shoulder and the base of her neck.

"Oh, God . . ." she said with a gasp. "Nicholas . . . oh, please, Nicholas."

She rolled back, pulled him atop her, and guided him inside. "I can't wait . . ." she said breathlessly. "Make love to me." She wrapped her long, lovely legs around his waist and pulled him down, deeper and harder into the firm, lovely moistness. "Make love to me," she cried. "Now!"

SEVEN

Carter brought Anita's bag over from the California after she promised to remain at the hotel. He half suspected that Yamun's people might try there again, and he warned her to be careful.

He just made it to the Sacré-Coeur as Belmont was pulling up in a Fiat convertible, the top up. Carter climbed in the passenger seat, and they headed out of Paris.

"Any trouble getting here?" Belmont asked.

"None. Did you expect any?"

The Frenchman shrugged. "I suspected Mademoiselle Gabrud might have insisted she come along."

Carter had to smile. Belmont was very good. One of the best in the business. "How did you know?"

"Come on, Nick—you forget this is my country."

"Sorry," Carter said. "She and I have an understanding."

"Oh?"

Carter explained what had happened at the hotel . . . all but the part about he and Anita making love. Belmont wouldn't understand it. Carter didn't think he did himself.

"You think he'll try again?" Belmont asked, alarmed.

"Not Yamun himself, but one of his people most certainly will."

"And you left her there?"

"She can handle herself. She's already shown that."

"Yes. I still have to figure out what I'm going to tell the chief of police. An Israeli citizen—a woman—kills an Arab and then throws his body down an elevator shaft." Belmont shook his head.

"Let's hope Yamun is at the farmhouse and we can get to him," Carter said.

Belmont looked at him. "He's there. I've got one good photograph. But it won't be that easy to get him."

Carter suspected his friend was correct, but he said nothing. Instead he sat back and relaxed. He lit a cigarette and watched the outskirts of Paris flash by.

Aubervilliers was a city of about a hundred thousand people. There was a lot of industry there, and yet the entire area was dominated by wheat fields and small farms, with patches of woods scattered here and there.

They went through the town and started out toward Beauvais, but they got less than two miles before Belmont turned off the highway and went down a narrow dirt road.

Within a couple of hundred yards they were stopped by a police barricade.

"Stay here for a moment, Nick," Belmont said. He got out of the car and went up to the police officers. He showed his credentials and then walked farther up the road through the woods.

There were a lot of cars and policemen there. The men were dressed in leather jackets, tall boots, and riot helmets, and carried submachine guns.

Carter did not like this. It felt all wrong. As if the entire place were going to go up in flames at any moment.

He opened the car door and got out. One of the policemen came up to him, shaking his head.

"*Non, non, monsieur,*" the policeman shouted.

Carter took out a cigarette and held it up without attempting to move away from the car. The cop stopped and nodded, then turned and went back up the road.

Carter could hear police radios crackling, and somewhere off to his right, in the woods, he could see a half-dozen policemen all standing around together. They were just at the crest of a hill, and they were looking down at something on the other side.

If the farmhouse was on the other side of the hill, and Yamun was actually still there, the police would have been spotted long ago.

Christ, they were all sitting ducks.

He lit the cigarette. He could see Belmont just up the road, standing in a knot of uniformed officers. It looked as if they were deep in some heated discussion.

One of the cops looked back toward Carter, then pointed, and Belmont looked up. He shook his head, and they went back to their conversation.

This was not going to work out very well, Carter thought. He didn't quite know why he felt it, but the instinct was very strong. Yamun was nearby, and he knew that they were here. He not only knew it, he was ready for them.

Belmont finally broke away from the group and came back to the car. Carter flipped his cigarette away.

"They are about ready to go in, Nick," the Frenchman said.

Carter glanced up again at the policemen in the woods. "I don't like this, Pierre. It's got a bad feel to it."

Belmont followed his gaze. "You may be right, but the operation is about to begin. You can stay here or come along."

Carter took a deep breath and let it out slowly. He pulled out his Luger, checked the action to make sure a shell was in the chamber, and nodded.

"Let's do it, then," he said.

By now most of the policemen had moved into positions up in the woods along the crest of the hill, on either side of the road, or in another assault group on the far side of the farm.

"There are helicopters standing by in case any of them slip through our net," Belmont said as he and Carter started up the road.

"Where's the weak link, Pierre?" Carter asked.

Belmont shrugged. "There is a small stream behind the house. He might make it undetected down there."

Carter was looking at all the men. They were practically climbing all over each other. "You know, he could come right through us. He could put on a uniform and we'd never pick him out."

"He would have to have a lot of courage. But it is possible, although we have the element of luck on our side."

Carter started to laugh, when the sound of automatic weapons fire came from above, in the woods. He and Belmont both instinctively crouched down and turned in that direction.

At least two men up on the crest had fallen, and the others were returning the fire.

"So much for our element of surprise," Carter said. He and Belmont, keeping low, zigzagged their way up the road, crossing into the woods just where the hill dipped down into a narrow gulley. The farmhouse, according to Belmont, was just on the other side.

The rattle of automatic weapons fire came sporadically now. It almost seemed as if whoever had fired first from the farmhouse had already given it up.

A low stone fence ran alongside the base of the hill, and Carter and Belmont ducked behind it as they came within sight of the old stone farmhouse. The house, along with several outbuildings, was on a flat spot about thirty yards on the other side of the fence.

From where Carter was crouched he could see cops in the fields and woods completely surrounding the house.

Someone raced from the back of the house toward the creek, and the woods behind the house erupted in a heavy curtain of small arms fire.

The man went down.

An instant later there was an oddly pitched crunch from the open door of one of the outbuildings.

"Down!" Carter shouted.

A couple of seconds later a tremendous explosion came from the hilltop, and police were screaming, trees were falling, and the smell of cordite hung in the air.

"Christ! A mortar!" Carter shouted.

He popped up and fired a half-dozen rounds in the vicinity of the storage shed.

The crunching sound came again, and he dove for the protection of the stone fence. He could hear the shell coming in, and then there was a huge explosion that lifted him right off the ground.

For at least a half minute Carter just lay there, stunned, his ears ringing, the smell of cordite very strong now.

Finally he managed to sit up. Belmont lay on his side in a heap, blood coming from his nose and ears, but his eyelids were fluttering. He was alive. A half-dozen policemen who had been crouching behind the fence about twenty-five feet away hadn't been so lucky, though. The mortar shell had evidently dropped right on top of them. Where the fence had been, there was nothing but a pile of pulverized rubble painted with blood, bits of bone, and scraps of clothing.

There was still some small arms fire from the crest of the hill, though it wasn't nearly as heavy as before. From the far side of the creek, behind the house, Carter could hear what sounded like a pitched battle.

He peered over the edge of the fence as the mortar was fired again, this time the shell going out toward the back, exploding seconds later in the woods.

He turned back to Belmont, who was just sitting up, holding his head.

"Are you all right, Pierre?" Carter asked.

Belmont looked up and nodded. "What the hell was it, Nick?"

"They've got a mortar in there. In the outbuilding on the west side of the house."

"*Merde*," Belmont said.

Carter looked over the top of the fence again. Police commanders up on the hill and on the far side of the creek were pulling their men together for an assault.

Now they were keeping their heads down, something they should have done in the first place. Every time Yamun or his people were underestimated, someone turned up dead, Carter thought. This had been going on for years, and still they did not learn.

The mortar fired, this time again from the front, the shell exploding up on the hill.

Carter had just seen a movement at the open window of the shed. He kept watching as he reloaded his Luger.

Belmont had managed to crawl up to the stone wall and look over. He too saw the movement.

"He's there. I saw him," Belmont said.

The mortar fired again, the round exploding up in the woods. Carter hoped the commanders had enough sense under this kind of attack to keep their men scattered.

"I'm going to have to take it out," Carter said, and as Belmont started to protest, he scrambled down to the fence, took one of the walkie-talkies from a dead officer, and brought it back. It seemed to be working. He gave it to Belmont.

"You can't go in there, Nick," Belmont said.

"Call your people and tell them I'm going in. I don't want to get shot in the back," Carter said.

Still another mortar round crunched out of the shed, this one toward the back again, aimed at the assault forces coming up from the creek. It meant whoever was doing the firing was momentarily looking that way.

Carter quickly scrambled over the top of the stone fence as Belmont got on the walkie-talkie to tell the police commanders what was about to happen.

The grass was fairly high for about five yards before it gave way to a patch of ground that had been plowed for planting but evidently had not been used.

Carter quickly made his way on his stomach to the edge of the bare patch, which ran completely across the front of the house as well as the outbuildings. If the no-man's-land hadn't been there to begin with, he suspected Yamun had ordered it made that way. It was a natural firebreak. No one could sneak up on him that way.

Another mortar shell crunched out toward the back, and the small arms fire that had been fairly heavy in that direction died down.

Evidently several of Yamun's people from the house had tried to make their way out back and had run into the assault forces.

Carter remained where he was, watching the outbuildings and the farmhouse itself for any sign of life. He held Wilhelmina up, its safety off, ready to fire if he saw the slightest movement. But there was nothing.

A second or two later, the mortar fired another shell up into the hillside. Carter tensed. If the pattern held, a second shell would be fired into the hill, and then the following two would be directed toward the back. It would be then that the no-man's-land in front would be clear . . . providing there was no one left in the farmhouse or the outbuildings watching out front.

A second shell lobbed up into the hillside. Carter counted five, then jumped up and, keeping low, raced across the open space, expecting at any moment to be fired upon.

The mortar fired toward the back, and a line of fire was laid down into the outbuilding from the hill.

The bare strip dipped down slightly, then rose up to the farmhouse. Carter made it to the edge of the sturdy stone building as the second mortar shell was fired toward the rear, and then he slipped around to the back.

He could see the creek and beyond, across a tall grass field, the woods. He could make out several policemen just within the protection of the trees. He hoped they had gotten Belmont's message via the walkie-talkie, because in just a moment he would become a clear target.

He took a deep breath, let it out slowly, and then raced along the back wall of the house just as the first mortar round exploded in the hillside out front.

He crossed the space between the farmhouse and the outbuilding, then eased around the corner to the edge of the front wall.

A second mortar round fired up into the hill, and Carter waited several seconds before he ducked around the corner. Holding himself tight, he leaped in front of the open window.

There were two men in the stone shed. In the middle of the room, set on a swivel, was a mortar, several cases of live shells stacked up on either side of it. One of the men was the aimer, and the other was just reaching for a shell.

"Hold it!" Carter shouted. The aimer spun around, pulling a pistol out of his belt.

Carter fired, the round catching the slightly built, dark-skinned man in the face, blowing off most of his left cheek and driving him backward to the rear window. A split second later the window exploded in a hail of automatic weapons fire from the police across the creek in the woods. The man's body did a macabre dance before it was flung forward on top of the mortar, knocking the weapon off its stand.

Carter leaped over the windowsill into the room as the second man charged. Carter shifted Wilhelmina to his left hand and smashed a roundhouse with his right into the second man's jaw, knocking him off his feet, over one of the cases of mortar ammunition.

Carter was on the second man an instant later, the muzzle of the Luger pressed firmly to his forehead.

The dead man was Arab. Probably Libyan. But this one appeared to be French.

He tried to struggle as he recovered until he realized his position, and then he slumped back.

"That is infinitely better, *monsieur*," Carter said in French. "Now tell me, where is Yamun?"

The man's eyes automatically flickered toward the rear door, but then he caught himself and looked back, shaking his head. "I don't know any Yamun," he said.

Yamun *had* been there after all!

"Belmont!" Carter shouted, turning his head toward the front window. "In here, Belmont!"

"Carter?" Belmont shouted from across the clearing.

"It's Yamun! He's escaped across the creek! Across the creek!"

Belmont shouted something else Carter didn't quite catch. Suddenly the Frenchman beneath Carter heaved up, shoving the muzzle of the Luger aside.

Carter was momentarily off-balance as the smaller man scrambled away. Before Carter could get to his feet, the Frenchman had reached one of the open cases of mortar ammunition, had grabbed a shell, and raised it high over his head.

"Now die, you bastard!" the crazed man screamed. He threw the shell.

Carter rolled left and leaped forward, just catching the shell before it could hit the stone floor and explode.

The Frenchman leaped for the front window and was halfway out when he was cut down by a hail of automatic weapons fire from the hill, blood erupting from his body as if it had exploded from within. And then he disappeared on the other side.

Carter just lay there, cradling the mortar round, his heart slowly beginning to ease its pounding in his chest

"Carter?" Belmont called. "Nick?"

"In here," Carter called.

A few seconds later, Belmont and a half-dozen officers appeared in the open window. Belmont took in the scene at a glance, and he grinned.

"Are you making love to the mortar?" he asked.

"It almost made love to me," Carter said. He sat up, gently laid the round aside, and then got to his feet as Belmont and the French police crowded into the small shed.

Belmont looked critically at him. "You are all right, my friend?"

"I'm fine," Carter said. He pulled Belmont outside. There were police everywhere. "What about Yamun?"

Belmont held up the walkie-talkie. "He got away, Nick."

"How?"

Belmont shook his head. "It was as you said it might be."

"We didn't have luck?"

"*Non*. They found the dead police officer. Without his uniform."

"Goddammit," Carter swore, looking away. "How in hell did he get away from the farmhouse and close enough to your lines?"

"I do not know, but he is gone now."

Carter looked back toward the dead man lying in front of the window. "That one is French. The one inside is Arab. Libyan, I'd suspect. Probably works at their embassy in town."

There were several policemen around the dead Frenchman. Belmont and Carter went over to the body. Belmont turned it over and looked at his face.

"Anyone recognize this one?" he asked the men.

They all shook their heads, but one did it more as a gesture of thoughtfulness.

"Yes?" Belmont said.

The officer looked up. "I do not know this man, Inspector, but he is from Marseille. I would bet anything on it."

"How do you know that?" Carter asked.

The policeman shrugged, the gesture typically Gallic. "I am from Marseille. And this man . . . has the look."

"*Merci*," Belmont said. He and Carter withdrew again. "So, what do you do now?"

"Back to the city. Yamun won't quit because of this. He'll try something else."

"I see," Belmont said. "I do not think I will be able to help much further, unless we get into it officially."

"I don't want that, Pierre. We'd stumble all over ourselves. Just like this today."

"I know. So I will stay out of it. But I am sure the

commissioner of police will want to thank you for this today. You have saved many lives.''

"I don't want any thanks," Carter growled. "I came to do a job, and it isn't done yet."

Belmont said nothing.

"Get me back to town, Pierre. I have a lot of work to do."

EIGHT

It was getting dark by the time Nick Carter made it back to the Lancaster. Belmont had dropped him off a couple of blocks from the hotel, and he had made it the rest of the way on foot.

The closer he got, the more he began to get nervous about Anita. Yamun was once again on the loose. There was no telling what he or his people would do now that their farmhouse cover had been blown and a lot of their troops killed.

He circled the hotel long enough to make certain that he had not been followed and that no one was hanging around watching, and he entered the lobby.

The police had left, and the hotel had gotten back to normal after the afternoon's excitement. Carter got his key from the desk and started toward the elevators, when the bell captain motioned him over to his station off to the side.

"You've been gone, so you don't know yet, I'm sure," the man said slyly.

"Know what?" Carter asked, starting to dig in his pocket for some money.

The bell captain held him off. "No tip necessary, *monsieur*. But I thought you should know before you went up that the business with your lady friend may cause you some trouble."

"Trouble?" Carter snapped. He glanced toward the

elevators. ''What are you talking about?''

'Two gendarmes came to get her just an hour ago. Maybe less.''

''Police? Uniformed cops?''

''No, sir. Detective inspectors.''

''How do you know . . .'' Carter started to ask, but he knew it was a silly question.

'They came to me, showed me their identification books, and asked me if the woman was still upstairs. I couldn't lie to the police.''

Carter turned, and ignoring the elevators, he raced up the stairs, taking them two at a time. He listened at his door, but there were no sounds from within, and he let himself in.

His room was in shambles. It did not look as if there had been any struggle, but his room had definitely been searched. The cassette radio in which he transported his weapons had been opened, but whoever had searched had not found the inner compartments. Wallpaper had been torn off the walls, light switches and wall plates taken off. The bed had been cut apart, and in the bathroom the toilet had been broken open. Water was everywhere.

Whoever had been there had been thorough. But what were they looking for? Did Yamun think that Carter had some specific information? Or had Yamun merely directed his people to search for anything that would give a clue as to Carter's identity?

The telephone had been torn apart so well he could not use it to call anyone. His clothes had been ripped up, as had his suitcase and overnight bag. There was nothing of value— either his or the hotel's—left behind.

Carter turned and left the room, going downstairs. Outside the hotel he hesitated just a moment. Yamun had given him a challenge. The man was drawing him forward. He wanted a confrontation, while at the same moment he was going to continue preparing for whatever it was he had come out for in the first place. He was certainly an arrogant bastard, Carter thought.

There was a telephone behind the bar at a small bistro a couple of blocks away. Carter gave the barman a few extra francs, and he dialed Belmont's private number. Belmont answered on the second ring.

"This is Carter."

"Yes, you are all right?"

"I need some information."

"I've already told you—" Belmont started, but Carter cut him off.

"Goddammit, Pierre, all I want is information!"

The line was silent for a moment. "All right, Nick. What is it you wish to know?"

"The Israeli woman who was with me. Anita Gabrud. She is missing. I was told she was arrested this afternoon by two men identifying themselves as police officers. I want you to find out if indeed she was arrested, and if so, where she is being held."

"Is that all?"

"What ship did those weapons at the farmhouse come in on?"

"The *Trader Princess*," Belmont said without hesitation. "Registered in Liberia, of course, but she's out of New York."

"That's where the weapons came from?"

"One can only guess, but I would guess not. Her last ports of call were Cairo and Tunis."

"In that order?"

"Yes."

"Then she passed just offshore of Libya. A fast boat out into the Med, load the weapons, and then Tunis, and here to Paris."

"Le Havre," Belmont said. "The ship's load was brought up from Le Havre on barges, of course."

"Where, exactly?"

"Many places within the city, depending upon the goods."

"But the weapons?"

"We don't know, Nick," Belmont admitted. "And that is all the information I have. I will find out about the woman. Where can you be reached within the next few minutes?"

Carter looked down at the phone and read off the number. Belmont hung up, and Carter ordered a cognac while he waited for his friend to call back. He lit a cigarette.

It was entirely possible, of course, that Anita was dead by now. He knew he should contact the Israeli embassy. Tell them what had happened. It was, after all, their problem.

But he and Anita had made love. They had something now that was far more than a casual working relationship.

The one thing Carter still could not figure was Yamun's use of the French underground. It simply did not make sense for an international terrorist of his experience and abilities to use relative amateurs. What was he trying to accomplish?

The telephone rang, and the barman answered it. He handed the telephone back to Carter. "It is for you, *monsieur*."

"Nick?"

"Yes. What did you find out?"

"She has not been arrested. But your hotel has already made a complaint about you. It seems you have done a lot of damage to your room. They would like to speak with you about restitution. The manager is very angry. He would like to have you arrested."

"I'll take care of it later, Pierre. Someone has come in and taken Anita. She was in my room. They searched it."

The line was silent.

"Hold the police off for a little while."

"I cannot, Nick," Belmont said. "If you formally ask for assistance, then I will be forced into acknowledging your presence. But if you wish to seek help with the police for your friend, then here is a name you must call . . ."

"No, thanks, Pierre. I won't bother you again."

"I am sorry it is turning out this way. But you must be very careful now. It is, I think, very dangerous for you."

"Thanks," Carter said. He hung up, finished his drink,

and left the bartender a few extra francs.

Outside he took a cab across the river to an area of waterfront hotels and clubs around the Paris heliport. The cabby wouldn't take him all the way into the section, but he let him off somewhere around the rue Camille Desmoulins. Carter had to walk the rest of the way.

The Café du Paris was a small dive that backed up to the river along a narrow, dirty street. A block farther along the riverfront drive were warehouses and docks for barges that brought cargo down from Le Havre 130 miles away. The area was bustling. There was a lot of traffic, lights lit the docks like day, and men worked unloading the barges.

According to Belmont, the ship was the *Trader Princess*. He'd probably find more information up in Le Havre, but the weapons almost certainly would have come to Paris by barge. And Anita had been taken from their hotel only a few hours ago, which meant it was likely she was still in or near the city. Carter guessed here in the waterfront district. He did not think Yamun had taken her himself. Most likely she had been taken by hoods from down here. If anyone knew anything, if there were rumors, they'd be floating around the bars down here.

Carter walked into the bar and ordered a cognac. Most of the men in the place looked like rivermen—rough, dirty, and mean. They did not like outsiders, and at first the barman did not want to serve Carter.

"I do not wish to play games with you," Carter said in street French. He shoved his money across the zinc bar. "A cognac. And be quick."

The barman nervously poured Carter's drink and set it in front of him. He scooped up the money as a burly, dark-haired riverman wearing a heavy checked coat came up the bar.

Carter glanced at him.

"Finish your drink, *monsieur*, and then get out of here," the big man growled.

Carter tossed back his cognac, shoved the glass forward, and laid down a fifty-franc note. "Another," he snapped. "And pour one for my friend here."

The big man reached out and grabbed Carter's arm, intending to shove him away from the bar. Instead Carter sidestepped, kicking the man in the ankle and at the same time hammering a short, very hard jab to the solar plexus.

It all happened so quickly and with so little fuss that only one or two others, including the bartender, even knew that anything was going on.

The breath had been knocked out of the big man. He stood there holding on to the edge of the bar, his face ashen.

"Our drinks," Carter said quietly to the barman, who hurriedly, and with a new respect, poured the cognacs.

Carter lifted his glass in a toast and drank it. "I came for some information," he said. "When I have it, I shall leave."

The big man eyed him. He slowly reached out for his drink, then tossed it back. He seemed to catch his breath. He smiled wryly. "You hit very hard, *monsieur*."

"I don't like being handled," Carter said. He nodded for another drink for both of them, then offered the other man a cigarette. The big man took one. Carter lit it, and then lit one for himself. He inhaled deeply.

For a minute or two nothing was said. The bar had gotten back to normal, and no one was paying them much attention. Finally the big man turned to look at Carter.

"You are an American," he said.

Carter shrugged.

"What sort of information do you want? And what sort of money would it be worth?"

The bartender had come a little closer. Carter looked pointedly at him, and the man turned and went over to the other end of the bar, out of earshot.

"It is very dangerous information," Carter said. "And I would be willing to pay plenty for it."

The burly riverman looked around. "The police would be interested? Are you police?"

"The police might be interested, but no, I'm no cop."

"Where, then, is the danger? What do you wish to know?"

"The *Trader Princess*. Have you heard of her?"

At the mention of the ship, the big man reared back almost as if Carter had waved a gun in front of his nose. His eyes widened, his nostrils flared. "*Merde,*" he muttered. He looked around. "That is very unhealthy to speak of, *monsieur*. It would be . . . very expensive information."

Carter withdrew a thousand francs from his pocket, and palming the bills so that no one else in the bar could see the money, he passed it over to the big riverman, whose eyes went even wider.

"It must be reliable information, *monsieur*," Carter said. "Lives will depend upon it. Especially yours."

"But if I say I cannot help you? What then?"

"I will leave you alone. There will be someone else willing to talk to me."

The big riverman made his decision. He took the money from Carter. "She came into Le Havre four days ago. She is due to ship out for New York City by midnight tonight."

Carter nodded. "There was cargo, brought here to Paris."

"There was much cargo," the big man said cautiously.

"A particular sort of cargo most interests me."

The riverman shrugged. He drank his cognac and puffed on the cigarette. He was beginning to sweat.

"This cargo would not have been delivered to the same place as the other merchandise. It would have been very secret. Very dangerous."

"*Oui*, it is very dangerous."

"It is the weapons I am interested in. The ship would have brought these weapons . . . perhaps for certain criminals . . ."

"La Pègre," the big man hissed.

"Where?" Carter asked urgently. *La pègre* literally meant the lowest of the low. Real scum. They were the worst of the criminal element within France.

"Very close," the riverman said. He named the warehouse. It was less than two blocks farther up river. "But there will be many eyes watching. You would not get close."

"*Merci*," Carter said. He finished his cognac, stubbed out his cigarette, and got up. He looked deeply into the big man's eyes. "It would not be wise for you to serve two masters, *monsieur*. Remain here, drink, and have a good time."

The riverman looked away. Carter glanced at the others in the bar, who were studiously ignoring him, and then he left, heading in the opposite direction of the warehouse controlled by La Pègre.

Within a half block, Carter knew that he was being followed. He walked in a large circle that would eventually bring him back to the river but that skirted the edge of the industrial area around the heliport.

Twenty minutes later he ducked down a narrow side street and stepped immediately into the deeper shadows of a doorway.

Moments later a tall, rat-faced man hurried around the corner, stopped a moment in confusion, and hurried up the street.

As he passed, Carter stepped out from the doorway. "Here I am," he said softly in French.

The rat-faced man stopped in his tracks and spun around, his right hand darting into his coat pocket and coming out with a knife.

Carter smiled. "You aren't being very sociable, my friend. I am just looking for a warehouse. Perhaps La Pègre might know . . ."

The man charged, but it was a fool's rush that Carter easily sidestepped. He chopped down on the man's knife hand, and the blade clattered to the pavement. The man was quick on his feet. He spun back, but Carter smashed his fist into the man's face, breaking his nose in a great spurt of blood and knocking him backward half into the street.

Carter turned back and scooped up his attacker's knife. In

the next instant the man was on top of him, a thin wire garrote around Carter's neck.

The knife clattered to the pavement once again as Carter was suddenly fighting for his life, the garrote cutting off his breath and the blood supply to his brain.

With incredible speed he could feel himself growing weak and dizzy as he tried to reach back for the man's head, or his shoulders, or anything to grab to throw the man off, but it wasn't working.

Carter was seeing spots and flashes in front of his eyes, and he started to go down, his knees becoming weaker, his legs giving way beneath him.

Now! He had to act now, or die!

Carter reached down behind his back, grabbed a handful of the man's crotch, and crushed with every ounce of his strength.

His assailant screamed and reared back, releasing his hold on the wire.

Carter shoved him off, yanked the wire away from his neck, and as he took huge drafts of sweet, cool air into his lungs, he turned back to the man who was moaning in the gutter.

"You bastard," Carter hissed, and he started to yank the Frenchman up. Suddenly the knife was coming at him. It must have been lying in the street.

Carter just managed to grab the man's knife hand, and with brute strength he stopped the thrust, turning it back and slowly but inexorably forcing the blade to the man's throat. And then, with a final push, he plunged the blade deep.

The Frenchman's body heaved, blood spurted up out of the open wound, and a terrible gurgling sound came from his chest as he drowned in his own blood.

Carter reared back, half stumbling, half falling, his throat terribly bruised by the wire.

At length he regained his balance, but for a moment he remained where he was. The rat-faced little man had followed him from the bar. That meant he had heard what went on between Carter and the riverman. It meant the riverman was in very big trouble.

For a few moments Carter debated with himself about going back to the bar. In the end he decided against it. The riverman had understood the risks better than Carter, an outsider, did. For now he would have to take care of himself. If they knew that someone was coming after them, La Pègre would be getting ready. The very least they would do would be to hide the evidence. If they were holding Anita, they would almost certainly kill her now.

Carter pushed away from the building and hurried down the narrow side street, back toward the riverfront warehouse district.

Five minutes later he could hear a siren in the distance behind him. He paused for a minute to listen. It came closer, but then it stopped.

It was possible that the body had been found already. He didn't think the police would do much about it, however. At least they'd be in no hurry to investigate the crime. Not at night. And not in this district.

He made it back to the main waterfront district, which was still busy with traffic, lights, and workmen unloading barges. This section of Paris never slept. There were almost always workmen down here. Paris was a big, hungry city. She had to constantly be clothed and fed. There were no holidays for that.

No one seemed to pay Carter any attention as he worked his way down to the warehouse that the riverman had told him about. The nearer he got, though, the rougher the district seemed to become.

The building itself was marked with a large, cracked, and faded sign over the main loading doors: MARCHAND IMPORTS.

There was a lot of activity on the docks, and a constant stream of forklifts and trucks came and went into the large warehouse.

The buildings on both sides were busy as well, but the warehouse two buildings to the west seemed deserted. Only a couple of security lights shone on the front.

Carter ducked back the way he had come, and he quickly worked his way around the block until he was just across a set of railroad tracks from the empty warehouse.

He hurried across the tracks, then around to the side of the building.

No one was there. A hundred yards to the east the dock was lit up and busy, but here was darkness.

Carter found a window, forced it open, and climbed in. He waited for several moments until he got his night vision back and then made his way to the rear of the building where he found stairs up to what had apparently once been the offices.

From there he made his way up a ladder to an access door to the roof. The view of Paris across the river was stunning from there, but he did not stop to look.

He hurried to the far side of the roof, climbed up over a tall brick wall, and dropped down to the next building's roof. He hurried across to the far side of that building and climbed over a similar brick wall.

On the other side he remained crouched where he dropped, suddenly aware that he was not alone.

That side of the roof was in nearly total darkness, but Carter could see that there were at least three armed men at the front edge of the roof, watching the street below. Another three were on the other side, watching the docks.

Somewhere between them, he figured there would have to be a way down.

He took three steps away from the brick wall, when it seemed as if the wall itself came down and smashed into the back of his head, and he watched as the roof came up to meet his face.

NINE

As he fought for consciousness Carter was dimly aware that he was being dragged down stairs, down a corridor, and finally across a carpeted floor.

He was propped in a chair, his hands and legs were tied, and he was left alone, the light very bright in front of his face, the rest of the room in darkness.

For what seemed a very long time he had trouble focusing his eyes, but then it all came together for him in a rush, and he raised his head.

"He is awake," someone called from behind.

"Nick?" A woman's voice came from the darkness. It was Anita.

"Are you all right?" Carter asked. He could see nothing beyond the strong light in his eyes. But he could hear someone coming behind him. It sounded as if it came from the corridor.

"I'll live," she said. She sounded weak.

"Help is coming," he lied.

"You called no one," a man said harshly in heavily accented English.

Carter looked up and could vaguely make out the darker outline of someone beyond the light.

"You're sure about that . . . ?" Carter asked, and someone behind him clapped his hands over the side of Carter's

103

head, the pain in his ears excruciating. The Killmaster strained against his bonds.

"I am quite sure about that, Monsieur Carter. Now I wish to know what you and this Israeli slut are doing here in Paris."

"It's our honeymoon," Carter said. He ducked his head, the expected blow from behind hitting the top of his skull, but not his ears.

The man behind him grabbed his hair and yanked his head backward.

"*Moment, Henri,*" the man in front said. He switched to English again. "We understand that she has come here looking for a certain gentleman for whom she has a vendetta. But you are a puzzle, *monsieur.*"

Carter remained silent.

"The woman I can understand. But you. Coming here with your weapons. You were at a certain farmhouse in Aubervilliers this day as well, from what I understand. Just who are you, *monsieur*? And who do you work for?"

"My name is Nick Carter. I work for Amalgamated Press and Wire Services."

"No!" the man shouted, and an instant later Carter could feel the wind of the blow that nearly landed on his ears again.

He allowed himself to relax slightly.

"You wish me to believe you are a newspaperman? It can easily be checked."

"Check it," Carter snapped.

"Why are you so heavily armed? A Luger, and a deadly-looking stiletto. It is not normal."

"This is a dangerous world we live in," Carter replied.

"You wish to kill this gentleman?"

"I wish to do a story about him. He should be very famous."

The man laughed. "You are a fool, *monsieur.* There will be only one story in your newspapers. It will be your obituary."

"It is the risk we all take," Carter said. "Even for you there is a risk."

"You will get to meet your friend, though I doubt he will be much interested in giving you the story you seek."

The blow to the side of Carter's head came again, the pain so terrible that he momentarily blacked out. When he came around he could only hear a ringing in his ears, under which he thought he could make out someone calling his name. But it came as if from a very long distance, and it was very faint.

He shook his head. The light was still strong. He could see no one else in the room. He managed to turn his head far enough so that the light was no longer directly in his eyes. He could see the corner of a table, and beyond it the edge of a doorway . . . open. No one was behind him now.

"Nick? Nick?" The voice was a little louder now. It was Anita.

He turned back to the light. "Anita?" he said in what he thought was a soft voice. He could barely hear himself.

"Nick, they're gone!" Anita said urgently. "We're alone." Her voice was coming back stronger now.

"Are you sure?"

"Yes, they're all gone."

"Where are you? I can't see you."

"Just to the right," she said. "Just a little to your right."

Carter jerked his chair to the right, nearly losing his balance but moving out of the area illuminated by the strong light.

He could make out Anita tied to a chair beside a large desk on which a gooseneck lamp was twisted up so that the bare bulb shone directly where Carter had been.

He listened, the sounds of the workmen in the warehouse below coming to him. He managed to scoot the chair around so that he was sideways to Anita and to the doorway that led through an outer office to the corridor. They were alone. The hoods had gone.

"Try to turn your back to me," he told Anita. "I'll get

closer. Maybe you can reach the knots holding my wrists and get me untied.''

"I'll try," she said, and she began rocking her chair back and forth, gradually turning herself around.

Carter slowly worked his way around the edge of the desk, moving barely an inch or so at a time. But ten minutes later the back of his chair was up against the back of hers, and she was able to reach the ropes holding his wrists.

"Can you get it?" he asked.

"I think so," she said.

Carter was facing the door. If their captors returned now, they would be finished. *A little longer*, he thought. *Just a little longer . . . .*

A minute later Carter could feel his bonds loosening, but at the same time he heard someone out in the corridor. It sounded like at least three or four men, and they were laughing about something.

Anita heard them as well, but she did not fumble with the knots. She kept working, and finally Carter's hands were free.

Four men came around the corner into the outer office as Carter fumbled in his trousers for Pierre.

"What is this . . .'' one of the men shouted, and they all rushed into the office.

"Hold your breath!" Carter said urgently over his shoulder to Anita. At the same moment he thumbed the trigger mechanism on the tiny gas bomb and lobbed it into the midst of the oncoming men.

The effect was nearly instantaneous. All four men reared back, their eyes suddenly bulging out as they tore at their throats in an effort to get air.

They slumped down, twitched, and then were still.

Carter counted a full thirty seconds before he let out his breath and cautiously tested the air. It was clear.

"It's all right now," he said to Anita as he quickly undid the bonds holding his legs.

"What was that?" she gasped, wide-eyed.

"Later," Carter said. When he was free he jumped up and started to untie Anita's bonds. The front of her blouse had been partially ripped off, exposing her breasts, which were cut and bruised. There was a large cut over her right eyebrow, and blood covered her left leg.

"Your weapons are over in the desk," she said. She looked to be in bad shape and was obviously just barely hanging on.

"What the hell did they do to you?"

She managed a wry smile. "They just asked me a few questions."

He had her untied, and she fainted in his arms. He placed her on the floor, then went to the desk, where he found Wilhelmina and Hugo in the top drawer. He slipped the stiletto into its chamois sheath on his right forearm, then checked to make sure the Luger was still loaded. It was. He levered a round into the firing chamber and then went to the four men sprawled grotesquely on the floor. He took the jacket off one of the bodies, walked back to Anita, and put it around her shoulders.

She came to as he lifted her, then Carter half walked and half dragged her to the door.

There was no one in the corridor, which opened at the far end on metal stairs that led down to the warehouse itself.

He stopped at the corner, then just eased himself around so that he could see what was going on below. The main floor was busy with dozens of men and at least a half-dozen forklifts scurrying back and forth from outside on the dock to a huge pile of pallets that seemed to contain some kind of machinery.

Out front, parked just beyond the open main doors, was a Citroën sedan. From Carter's vantage point, he could see no one in it or even nearby.

Carter figured it probably belonged to the one who had questioned him. He did not think Yamun would show up here in such an ostentatious manner.

A door slammed behind him, and Carter spun around in

time to see a short, stocky man starting down the corridor.

Anita stiffened in his arms. "It's him," she whispered. "The one who questioned me."

The corridor light was dim, and Carter and Anita were in the shadows by the stairway. Their interrogator never saw them until it was too late.

Carter stepped around the corner, bringing the Luger up so that it was pointed directly at the man's face. "Make a noise and you're dead," he said softly.

Their interrogator started to step back, his complexion paling, but then he thought better of it. He slowly raised his hands over his head.

Carter stepped away from the stairwell, still helping a very weak Anita to stay on her feet. "We're going to leave in your nice car. Together. With no trouble."

"You will not get out of Paris alive, *monsieur*," the man said. "This is my city."

Carter grinned. "You may not get out of this building alive."

The man glared at him.

"Will you tell me where I can find Yamun? Or will I have to take you with me and convince you to tell me?"

"He is here in Paris."

"Where?"

"I do not know, *monsieur*." The man shrugged. "He is in hiding. He is just here, that is all."

"What if you want to contact him? How do you do it?"

The husky man grinned sardonically. "One does not contact him . . . it is he who reveals himself."

Anita had lost some blood, and she was pretty well beat up. Carter figured he was going to have to get her someplace where she could receive some medical attention, and very soon.

"One more thing," Carter said. "Why has Yamun supplied La Pègre with weapons?"

"You are from the police," the man hissed. He took a step forward, and Carter almost shot him.

"I am not from the police, *monsieur*. In this you must believe me. And I have no interest in your dealings other than how they will lead me to Yamun."

"He is just a broker. The weapons are not for . . . Paris."

"Then for whom? For Yamun? What is he planning?" Carter snapped. He could not remain there much longer.

The Frenchman read something of Carter's desperation. "Please, *monsieur*. The weapons are merely in transit here."

"For where?"

The man began to squirm. "He will kill me."

"Or I will here and now."

Anita came half awake again and she lurched, pulling Carter temporarily off-balance.

The La Pègre chief took advantage of the momentary opening, and he shot forward, batting the barrel of the Luger aside. Anita slumped to the floor. In the next instant the Frenchman had Carter's neck in a stranglehold.

"*You* will be the one to die now," he rasped.

Carter drove his knee up toward the man's groin, but the Frenchman was a man of the streets, and he deflected the blow with his thigh as he tried to twist Carter's head far enough to break his neck.

For the second time that evening Carter found himself fighting for his life, consciousness beginning to fade.

He dropped his Luger, the weapon clattering to the floor, then managed to shove the Frenchman around so that his back was against the wall. He hammered a blow into the man's side, and the Frenchman grunted. Carter hammered a second and a third shot to the man's ribs, each time forcefully expelling air from the Frenchman's lungs.

The grip on Carter's neck loosened enough for him to pull free, struggle back, and get his stiletto into his palm.

The Frenchman charged, Carter sidestepped, and then he was on the man, the point of the razor-sharp blade inches from his eye.

"Where are the weapons going?"

The Frenchman tried to struggle. Carter shoved the point

of the blade three-quarters of an inch into the man's eyeball, while at the same time he clamped his left hand over the man's mouth. He immediately withdrew the blade, the Frenchman struggling wildly in his grip.

"The next time it goes all the way into your brain," Carter growled. "Where do the weapons go next?"

"New York! New York!" the Frenchman cried when Carter removed his hand.

"How?"

"By Air France. Tomorrow. Tomorrow!"

"What flight?"

"I don't know . . . it is the one that lands at Kennedy in the late morning. It is all I know! I swear!"

It didn't make any sense to Carter. In the first place, why would Yamun work with such scum? In the second place, why would the weapons have been dropped off in Paris for a flight to New York, when the ship they had come in on was herself bound for New York?

He was missing something. He could almost feel it around the edges. He knew damned well he was missing one fact, one detail, one little idea that would explain it all.

Carter focused on the underworld chief. He did not think the man knew anything more. Yamun wouldn't have told him anything else. Certainly nothing about his real plans.

"Listen to me very carefully now, *monsieur*," Carter said. "Your life will depend upon it."

The Frenchman nodded very carefully. His destroyed eye gave him a monstrous look.

"We are going to leave now, with you, in your car. You will guarantee us our safe passage. And after we are clear of the district, we will let you go, I promise you. I want you to bring a message to Yamun. Do you understand?"

"You will not let me live!"

"Oh, yes, I will. I want you to take a message."

"I cannot reach him."

"You can. There is something wrong with the shipment of weapons. You will reach him with my message."

"What message?"

"Tell him that his sister deserved to die!"

The man paled.

"I'm waiting to meet the coward who let it happen to his own flesh and blood. He is no man. He is only a killer of young boys."

"I cannot . . ."

"You will," Carter said softly, raising the stiletto toward the man's other eye. "It is the only way he will let you live for allowing us to escape. You will tell him, and he will be so enraged with the thought of getting to me, he will forget about you."

Carter roughly shoved the Frenchman aside, then quickly scooped up his Luger. He wiped his blade on his handkerchief, then sheathed it. The Frenchman was watching him carefully with his good eye.

"You can either live to take the message to Yamun . . . or you can die right now trying to stop me," Carter said.

The Frenchman nodded. "I will help you. Only because I wish to see the look on Yamun's face when he tells me how he will deal with you. He does not kill in a pretty manner."

"*Bon*," Carter said. He gently helped a partially conscious Anita to her feet, and keeping the Luger hidden at his side, he motioned for the Frenchman to pass them and go down the stairs.

"I will not hesitate to kill you," Carter said.

"It will not be necessary," the man said. He carefully stepped around Carter and Anita, and holding a hand to his damaged eye, he started down the stairs, Carter supporting Anita directly behind him.

No one below paid them the slightest attention until they had nearly reached the bottom. Forklifts went back and forth, some with huge, tall loads. Workmen were busy loading and unloading pallets.

A man in a chauffeur's uniform had been talking with one of the workmen. He looked around, then started across the warehouse.

The Frenchman waved him back.

"Who is he?" Carter asked.

"My chauffeur."

The man stopped, confused.

"Is he armed?"

The Frenchman hesitated.

"Is he armed?" Carter demanded.

"Yes . . . yes, he has a weapon."

"If he approaches us, you are a dead man," Carter said. "*Allons!* To your car!"

They slowly started across the floor of the warehouse toward the large open doors at the front. The chauffeur knew something was wrong. He started to reach inside his coat pocket, but again the La Pègre chief gestured him back.

Some of the workmen, suddenly realizing that something was happening, stopped what they were doing. They fell back as their boss and the man and woman passed.

Three quarters of the way to the door, the Frenchman stopped. All activity in the warehouse had ceased. The Citroën was just beyond the door.

"Where will you take me?"

"Into the city," Carter said. "I have given you my word that you will not be harmed. I want you as a messenger boy."

"How do I know . . ."

"You don't," Carter hissed. He stepped close behind the man and brought the Luger up, pressing the muzzle into the man's back. "Move," he said.

A ripple of dark murmurs crossed the warehouse, but no one made a move.

Anita was beginning to come around again as they reached the front doors and stepped out into the bright lights overhead.

"Open the rear door," Carter snapped.

The Frenchman did as he was told, then stepped back as Carter awkwardly helped Anita inside while keeping the Luger trained on their passport out of the district.

When she was in the back, he closed the door, then opened

the front passenger door. "Inside," he ordered.

The Frenchman complied and scooted behind the wheel. Carter got in and closed the door as the La Pègre chief, sweating furiously now, started the engine.

The doorway of the warehouse was lined with his men.

"Move it!" Carter said.

With a last sideways glance at his stronghold, the Frenchman slammed the car in gear, and they took off into the night, Carter directing.

They followed the Seine up past the Eiffel Tower, finally crossing over at the Place de la Concorde, where Carter had the man turn immediately right toward the Louvre, then pull over two blocks later.

When they were stopped, Carter looked into the man's eyes. "You will not forget my message to Yamun?"

"No, I will not forget. Neither will he."

"Get out," Carter said.

The Frenchman took a long last look at Carter, then got out of the car and immediately crossed the busy boulevard at a break in traffic.

Carter slid over behind the wheel, and before the Frenchman was all the way across, he took off into the night.

TEN

Pierre Belmont lived in a very old, very expensive house in the Marais district near the Place des Vosges. It was very late when Carter drew up past his place, then continued two and a half blocks farther. He parked the big car in a narrow, dark alley, then helped Anita out of the back seat.

"Nick?" she asked, only dimly aware of what was happening around her.

"We're all right now," he said soothingly. "It's safe here."

There was no traffic on these streets, so Carter was easily able to walk the Israeli woman back up to Belmont's home. He went to the side service entrance and rang the bell.

He heard a dog barking somewhere nearby, and in the distance, back toward the city's center, he could hear an ambulance. Paris, like any large city, never slept.

Carter rang the bell again, and the overhead light came on. Belmont's voice came through the speaker grille.

"What is it?"

"Pierre. It's me, Carter. There has been some trouble."

There was a very long silence. Carter was about to ring the bell again, when the door lock snapped and the door swung open. Pierre Belmont, in a bathrobe and slippers, a big Colt .45 automatic in his hand, the hammer cocked, stood there scowling.

"Is that the Israeli woman?" he asked.

"She's hurt."

"Who did this?"

"La Pègre," Carter said. Belmont made no move to allow them in. "It's not for me, Pierre. I'm leaving. It is for her."

"Israeli doctors are some of the best in the world. Take her back to her embassy."

"I can't. Not while Yamun is on the loose."

"Merde," Belmont said.

"Pierre?" a woman called from within the house. It was his wife. She had never liked Carter; he and what he represented threatened the security she felt her husband should be able to provide for her.

"I want you to take care of her. I will leave immediately."

"You will leave France?"

"For now."

"For how long, Nick?"

"Pierre . . . ? Who is there? What is happening? It is late," his wife called again.

"I don't know how long I'll be gone," Carter said. "But she needs help, and I can't have her going back to her own people. Not just now."

"Because of the leak?"

"Exactly."

Madame Belmont was at the door. "What is it, Pierre?" she asked, but then she saw who it was. "Carter . . ." she started. In the next moment, however, she realized that Carter was holding a gravely injured woman. *"Mon Dieu!"* she cried.

Carter stepped back as the door swung open.

"What has happened? Who is this?" the woman asked as she helped Carter bring Anita into the house past a bewildered Belmont.

At the stairs, Anita came around sufficiently so that Madame Belmont could manage her on her own. They went upstairs while Belmont led Carter back to his study and poured them both a stiff shot of cognac.

"You look like hell, Nick," Belmont said. "What happened?"

Carter quickly explained to his SDECE friend what had gone on that afternoon and evening from the time he had returned to his hotel and had found Anita missing.

"That would be Paul Gide," Belmont said. "He is a very powerful man in Paris. You say he has some connection with Yamun?"

"Apparently."

"There were some of Gide's people at Aubervilliers, at the farmhouse. But we thought they might have been involved out of territorial courtesy to the Le Havre people. It is not the sort of thing Gide usually involves himself with."

"What, then?"

"Cocaine, heroin . . . sometimes the horses . . . a few clubs, prostitution . . . and, of course, his shipping business."

"But no guns."

"Not usually," Belmont said thoughtfully. "Nor has he ever had a foreign connection as such, at least not to my knowledge."

"He has now."

Belmont nodded. He drained his snifter, then got the bottle and poured Carter another, and himself more. "So what do you want us to do for you, my friend?"

"Take care of Anita for a couple of days. At least until you hear from me."

"And if we do not . . . hear from you?"

"Then in a couple of days get her to her embassy. This Gide will be looking for both of us. It would not do for her to be caught alone on the street."

"I thought you said she was very capable."

"She is. The odds are just a little high."

Again Belmont nodded thoughtfully. "And you will return to New York? To meet the Air France shipment?"

"Right," Carter said. "I'm asking that you not say anything, Pierre. I want that shipment to go through so that I can find out where it's going.''

"I hadn't intended on telling anyone, Nick. It would necessitate me answering some very embarrassing questions. No, you will have your way.''

"Thanks," Carter said. He glanced toward the door. ''I do expect she's going to be a very unpleasant guest when she wakes up and finds out I've left her behind.''

Belmont smiled. ''Do not underestimate the power of my wife, Nick.''

"Thank you . . . again, my old friend.''

"Yes," Belmont said, nodding. ''I am a man destined to live the same experience over and over again.''

Carter finished his drink, then went to the door. ''After a while you should begin to get pretty good at it.''

Belmont got dressed and drove Carter to the American embassy on the Avenue Gabriel. They shook hands. ''Take care, Nick,'' Belmont said. ''I want you to come back for your charge.''

"Thanks, Pierre. Thanks a lot.''

Belmont shrugged, and Carter got out of the car, hurried across the walk, and went in past the guards on the strength of his identification.

He did not want to bother the ambassador, so he got the CIA chief of Paris station out of a party with friends. The man arrived forty-five minutes later, in a tuxedo, out of breath and red-faced.

"This had better be good," he said.

Carter nodded. ''I need an encrypted line to Washington. And I'll need transportation back to the States—tonight. Preferably something fast . . . *very* fast.''

"Just who the hell do you think you are, mister?'' the station chief asked. He was a man in his early fifties, Carter figured. A former Army colonel, if he remembered correctly . . . not used to taking orders.

"I'm in the middle of a very delicate operation here. Sooner or later you'll call Washington for confirmation of just who I am. If you do it now, you'll save yourself a lot of embarrassment, sir.''

The man's name was Howard DeVries. He looked hard at Carter now. He was no amateur. He nodded. ''I think we'd better do just that.''

Carter followed him downstairs to the communications room and had a cup of coffee while he waited. Twenty minutes later DeVries came out.

''Mr. Carter? Washington is on the line for you, sir.''

Carter went into the crypto center with the CIA chief. Some of the electronic machines had been covered with blankets. Carter was directed to sit at a desk where the phone was waiting for him. It was a direct circuit with Langley. It took less than five minutes to patch the call over to Hawk's number. In the meantime, DeVries was on another telephone, arranging for a military flight back to the States.

''Are you all right?'' Hawk asked.

''I'm coming to New York,'' Carter said. He explained what happened.

''And you say the Gabrud woman is at Pierre Belmont's home?''

''Yes sir.''

There was silence on the line for a moment. Carter could visualize the AXE chief chewing on his cigar. ''All hell has broken loose in Tel Aviv and here in Washington because of her. The State Department has been told you have either kidnapped her or killed her.''

''We'll have to hold them off a little longer, sir.''

''You're sure about this leak from Aman or the Mossad to Yamun?''

''Not one hundred percent, but it would explain a lot that has happened.''

''Yes, sir.''

''Yes,'' Hawk said. ''What about the Air France shipment into New York? The guns are evidently for Yamun's people.''

''I don't know, sir,'' Carter said. His mind was racing to a dozen different possibilities, not one of them really satisfactory.

"The transshipment with Paris as an intermediary could have been merely a diversion," Hawk said. "Something to muddy the trail."

"Yes, sir. It's possible. And yet it exposed whatever Yamun is planning to another risk. It's just not like him."

"Follow the shipment in New York. I'll make sure the port authorities keep away. Do you want some backup?"

"I think not, sir. There'll be more chance of success if I do it alone."

"I agree," Hawk said.

"But I would like you to do one thing for me, sir."

"What's that?"

"Set up surveillance on the Libyan delegation in Washington."

"That can be arranged. Anything else?"

"Have the Libyan delegation to the U.N., up in New York, watched as well."

"Do you think Qaddafi is behind this?"

"It's possible, sir. I just don't know. This is starting to make no sense to me. And when Yamun is involved, that is a very dangerous state of mind to be in."

"He'll come gunning for you sooner or later, N3."

"I hope so. But somehow I don't think he will. He's too much the professional for it. He'll save me until after his operation."

"You may be right," Hawk said. "Is there anything else?"

"I'll need clothes and luggage, another cassette recorder for my weapons, and I'll need another gas bomb and more nine-millimeter ammunition."

"I'll have it waiting in New York for you."

"Thank you, sir."

"Good luck."

DeVries was waiting for Carter out in the corridor. He seemed somewhat agitated.

"How about my transportation?"

"We're going to have to get you out to Bagnolet Air Force Base. A B-58 Hustler is on its way from Ramstein Air Force Base in Germany. The French have agreed to let it land to pick up a passenger, but then it must leave immediately. It won't even be allowed to refuel."

"Have you transportation for me to Bagnolet?"

"I'll drive you out there myself," DeVries said. "But would you mind telling me what's going on?"

"Sorry," Carter said. "Shall we go?"

DeVries looked at him. "I suppose I could pull some strings . . ." he began. He shook his head. "But I don't imagine I'd get a thing except a slap on the wrist."

"Something like that," Carter replied, grinning.

It took less than forty minutes for the trip out to the French air base east of Paris. They were allowed through the gate after they showed their credentials, and a call was made to the operations officer.

The deadly B-58 Hustler sat in the middle of the apron, isolated from any other aircraft or buildings but surrounded by French military police and vehicles. The pilot was leaning against one of the jeeps, off to one side, smoking a cigarette.

Carter was provided with a helmet and flight suit, shook hands with the CIA chief of Paris station, and then was driven out to the aircraft.

Major John Dunbar, a wing commander out of Ramstein, was his pilot. He had been told nothing except that he was to transport a VIP to New York. No questions were to be asked.

He and Carter shook hands, and they climbed up into the aircraft. Within five minutes the engines were started, the preflight check was completed, and they took off into the brilliant night sky, all of Paris laid out beneath them and swiftly falling behind as they screamed west in excess of a thousand miles per hour.

It was a little after three in the morning, Paris time, when they lifted off and barely 3:00 A.M., East Coast time, when they touched down at McGuire Air Force Base east of Phila-delphia. They had beaten the sun by a few minutes, and Carter felt as if he had run the entire distance. He was very tired, and his muscles were cramped from sitting in the cockpit.

Brad Williams had brought up his luggage, clothing, the cassette recorder, extra ammunition, and a new gas bomb, plus an Air France maintenance worker's coveralls.

They went over to the BOQ where Carter took a quick shower, shaved, and then got dressed. A pot of coffee and a platter of steak and eggs were sent up, and as he wolfed the food down, Williams filled him in on the operation to date.

"There's been quite a bit of activity in Washington," he said. "It seems as if damned near every Libyan has left the city."

Carter looked up. "What?"

"That's what we hear. They've all come up here, to New York, for the most part."

"Why? Any ideas?"

"One big one. The colonel himself may be coming over in two days to speak to the United Nations."

"He'd want his supporters on hand. But why speak now?"

"It's probably because of the President's State of the Union address. It takes place on the same day."

"To a joint session of Congress?"

"Right. It's got half of Washington in a tizzy. No one can miss the President's talk, of course, and yet to see Qaddafi here in the States is almost too tempting to pass up."

"The weapons are being shipped here, to New York."

"Could Qaddafi be planning something?" Williams asked.

"You're damned right he's planning something, and Yamun is his chief architect."

"But what? Some kind of a disturbance here in New York at the same time the President is speaking in Washington?"

"Evidently. But whatever it's going to be, it'll be big, you can count on it."

"I don't like this," Williams said.

"Neither do I, Brad. How about the Libyans all packing into New York? Any word as to what they've been up to?"

"Keeping quiet, mostly. The usual cocktail parties, of course. But everyone seems to be behaving himself, waiting for their glorious leader."

Carter had finished eating. He poured himself another cup of coffee and lit a cigarette. "Did you find out when the Air France flight comes in?"

"Right," Williams said. He consulted a notebook and read off the information, including the access code for the security door lock that would let him get down to the flight line. "Your badge is on the coveralls. You won't be stopped unless it's by Yamun's people who may recognize you."

"Comforting," Carter said. He glanced at his watch. He still had plenty of time to drive up to Kennedy Airport and get ready.

"Anything else you want done?" Williams asked.

"Yeah. Get back down to Washington, and have Becker at State supply us with a list of every known Libyan who lives in or around the city."

"New York?"

"No, Washington," Carter said. Something way at the back of his brain was telling him to be careful, to be very careful.

"Then what?" Williams asked.

"I want them tracked down. If they're in New York, I want to know."

"If they're in Washington?"

"I want them watched."

Williams shook his head. "Do you realize the manpower that'll take, Nicholas, my boy?"

"Plenty," Carter said. "State should be able to help, and so can the FBI. Hawk will pull the strings."

"Give me two guesses," Williams said. "You want this done immediately and very quietly."

"You're learning, limey, you're learning!"

The sun had risen and shone brilliantly on the Lower Bay

as Carter drove over the Verrazano Narrows Bridge from Staten Island into Brooklyn, following the Shore Parkway past the Aqueduct Race Track and finally around to JFK International Airport. Traffic had started out light, but now it was very heavy. The planes had begun taking off, thundering out across Jamaica Bay, for all parts of the world. Other planes were coming in. With whom? Or, rather, with what?

He stopped to pull on his coveralls before the airport. His pass identified him as an airport supervisor. No one would stop to question him, least of all any Air France employee. The airlines played it very straight with airport supervisory personnel. They could not afford to do otherwise.

There was a security sticker on the windshield of the car Williams had provided him with, so he had no trouble getting onto the employees' parking lot.

It was a warm morning, the air smelling of a combination of the tidal flats and spent jet fuel. He lit a cigarette as he walked across to the international terminal and entered by one of the maintenance doors.

The security guard looked up, spotted Carter's pass, then nodded and went back to his *New York Times*.

Carter went through the terminal to the Air France gates, then let himself through the door and went downstairs to the arrival area.

He checked his watch as an Air France 747 came in from the east for a landing. He smiled. He had just made it on time.

Two Air France ground crewmen came out of the building, glanced idly at Carter, and then moved off to the parking area.

Carter slipped inside the break room. The lounge's window overlooked the arrival area where the aircraft would be unloaded. There were a half-dozen Air France employees waiting. Carter got himself a cup of coffee, and one by one the others straggled outside for the arrival of the first morning flight.

He stepped over to the window, and keeping well back so that he would be less conspicuous to anyone around the plane, he watched.

A six-car baggage-handling train came around the corner and parked off to one side. Next, a truck on scissors lifts came up. It contained the janitorial crew as well as the food handlers.

The gigantic 747 suddenly appeared from around the corner of the terminal and was directed to a gate area. The Air France crew swarmed over the plane as soon as she was stopped and her engines began to wind down.

The big doors covering the aircraft's hold were swung open, and Carter put down his coffee cup.

The baggage train came up, and suitcases and other boxes and crates were pulled out of the belly of the plane.

At that moment a truck marked National Imports, Bayonne, N.J., pulled up and backed to the hold.

Two men jumped out and showed their bills of landing, and soon a dozen obviously heavy crates were being loaded onto the truck. Even from inside the break room, Carter could easily read the legend on the sides of the crates.

Marchand Imports.

Bingo, he thought.

ELEVEN

Nick Carter waited until the truck had been loaded and headed away before he left the break room, hurried back through the terminal, and raced back outside to where he had parked his car.

If the weapons were being taken to the National Imports warehouses in Bayonne, which he expected they were, then the truck would take the same parkway out across Staten Island that he had come in on. From there they'd go up on the Willowbrook Expressway.

He had to slow down for the automatic barrier to rise at the exit, but then he was speeding along the back road that led out to the parkway, the airport behind him and to the right.

The highway rose up on his right, and for a mile or so the road Carter was on remained below the parkway, separated by a tall, wire mesh fence.

He spotted the National Imports truck ahead of him on the main highway, and he sped up, passing it just before the access road curved sharply to the right and led onto the highway.

There was a lot of traffic now. He gradually worked his way over to the far right lane and slowed down, constantly watching in his rearview mirror for the white truck, which finally caught up.

He eased over to a center lane as the truck started to pass on the left lane, and he matched speeds.

The truck was much taller than his car, so Carter could not see the driver. But he could see the man in the passenger seat. He was a swarthy, dark-haired man, and unless Carter completely missed his guess, Libyan.

Carter took out his Luger and snapped the slide back. The passenger in the truck glanced down as Carter brought up the gun. The man's eyes went wide.

"Pull it over!" Carter shouted above the road noise.

The passenger turned and shouted something at his driver. A second later the driver leaned over so that he could see what was going on.

Carter gestured with his gun for the driver to pull over.

The truck sped up and pulled sharply over to the right directly toward Carter, who slammed on his brakes as the big truck's rear bumper flashed by.

Brakes screeched behind him, and a horn blared. Carter glanced in the rearview mirror, spotted a break in the traffic, and came up behind the truck on the left side. There was plenty of room here for him to run off the road with no real danger.

His passenger-side window was open. The truck's rear double tires were just coming even with the window when he raised the Luger and snapped off a single shot.

Immediately he jammed on his brakes as the truck shot forward, then lurched sharply right and sharply left, running two cars off the road, smoke and big pieces of the disintegrating tires flying everywhere.

For a second or two Carter thought the driver would regain control of the truck, but then it careened wildly to the left, bumped down off the apron, crossed a shallow ditch, and then sideswiped the tall fence, the wire mesh peeling off the uprights like a banana skin.

Carter turned off the road at the same moment the truck's front right tire hit a sinkhole, and the truck suddenly skidded to the right and flipped over.

Ignoring the traffic, Carter jammed the accelerator pedal to the floor, shot back out onto the highway, and flashed past the truck just as a huge fireball shot straight across the road. A split second later the concussion wave hit, and Carter was suddenly going sideways, his car completely out of control.

He braced himself for the crash as he careened off the side of another car, then skidded off the road and across the ditch, the car rising up on its side and finally slamming into the fence.

He was out of the car in seconds, racing back toward the furiously burning truck. A huge explosion sent pieces of burning wreckage high into the sky and across the road. A grass fire had begun on the far side of the wire mesh fence. Carter could hear the sounds of small arms ammunition popping off. The cab of the truck was completely engulfed in flames. Even from a distance the heat was intense.

Carter holstered his Luger. There would be nothing to learn back there. The truck was gone, as were its driver and passenger.

He turned back. A lot of cars had pulled over on the highway, the drivers out looking at the accident.

This arms shipment had been stopped, and there was no information to be gained here. But perhaps there had been other shipments. Someone at National Imports in Bayonne would know something. It was a possibility.

Yet once they found out what had happened here, they'd run.

Carter raced back up to the road and across to a convertible. The driver had gotten out of his car and had walked back about twenty yards.

He stepped aside as Carter ran past him and leaped into the car.

"Hey!" the driver shouted.

The engine was still running. Carter slammed the car in gear and took off.

"Hey!" the driver screamed. "Son of a bitch!"

Traffic had slowed way down for the first half mile or so

because of the fire behind them, but after that the Shore
Parkway was back to normal.

He made very good time, weaving in and out of traffic all
the way up to the Willowbrook Expressway and then across
on the Bayonne Bridge. Past the New Jersey Central railroad
tracks, he turned off the main drag and headed back toward
the waterfront on the New York side.

This was a fairly rough neighborhood. Just the sort of place
he had expected the warehouse to be in.

He stopped near the bay, across from the Naval Supply
Depot, at a corner where a couple of old winos were standing
and talking. He motioned them over to the car. He held up a
couple of tens.

"I'm looking for National Imports. Where do I find it?"

The winos looked at each other. One of them grabbed the
money and nodded over his shoulder. "Out on the Hook," he
said.

"What're you talking about?"

"The Hook, goddammit. Constable Hook. Turn around,
go back a couple of blocks, then hang a left. Down on the
wharves. You can't miss it." The drunk laughed.

"Thanks," Carter said. He spun the car around and raced
back a couple of blocks, easily finding the street that led out
to the docks.

The neighborhood was even shabbier than the rest of
Bayonne. Huge sections of the streets were torn up, buildings
were either falling down or boarded up, and everything as far
as the eye could see was littered with debris of every sort. The
neighborhood seemed deserted, too. There weren't any
people, and there was no traffic.

Carter pulled up a half block from a four-story brick
building that stood alone at the water's edge. Two rickety
wooden docks jutted well out into the bay. From there he
could see the far end of the Naval Supply Depot docks across
the way.

A big sign on the side of the building read: NATIONAL
IMPORTS OF BAYONNE.

Carter checked his Luger, then got out of the car, pocketed the key, and started toward the warehouse on foot.

There were a lot of windows on the front of the building, but they were all painted over. On the far side the delivery driveway led back to the big service doors and loading docks. There was no one back there. Nor was there anyone in sight on the docks themselves.

To Carter this smelled like a setup. But it was one he could not ignore. If the Libyans were planning on starting something here in New York when Qaddafi arrived, he wanted to know about it.

A big boat hooted out on the bay as Carter jumped up on the loading docks and stepped just within the warehouse. There were a lot of crates piled up on row after row of pallets. There was a lot of money in merchandise sitting here in the open without a guard.

Carter pulled out his Luger and flipped off the safety. He skipped across an aisle and stopped short within the shadows behind a stack of crates. He studied the labels of the boxes. There were canned hams from Denmark, some wine from France, and farther back in this row, there were more crates from Marchand Imports.

More guns.

Carter rapped on the top crate of a short pile. Then he shoved against it. The big box moved easily. It was empty. It meant the weapons had already arrived and had already been distributed.

But where? Here in New York as he was being led to believe? It was too damned pat. If Yamun was involved, and apparently he was, there was definitely something more to this business than was apparent on the surface.

Carter turned the corner and started down one of the back rows of crates toward the front of the building, when the big service doors rumbled shut, plunging the warehouse into darkness.

Carter slipped down another aisle, then circled back toward the center of the main storage area.

There was someone to his left and behind him, as well as over toward the service doors.

Carter holstered his Luger, his eyes now becoming accustomed to the darkness so that he could at least see some shadows, and climbed up on a crate. From there, very carefully and very quietly, he continued up the stack, working his way higher and higher, and closer to the service doors.

He stopped at one point and held his breath as someone hissed below. A moment later someone answered with the same sound toward the doors.

Carter continued to the edge of the pile, then flattened himself against the crates. He took out Wilhelmina. There were two men crouched by the service doors. A third was directly below, peering around the corner, and Carter was certain he could hear two others in the back rows.

He looked back the way he had come, a tiny sound catching his attention, in time to see the vague silhouette of a man climbing up on the pile of crates.

Keeping flat, Carter scrambled carefully off the side of the pile he was on, working his way down into the stacks.

Again he holstered his Luger, and this time he slipped out his stiletto. Unless he could get them all in one spot at the same time so he could use his gas bomb as he had in Paris, he'd have to pick them off one by one.

The razor-sharp blade gleamed dully in the dim light as Carter held it at the ready.

Suddenly he could hear the man breathing a couple of feet away, and just above. The stack of crates swayed slightly. Carter tensed. There could be no noise.

The man was directly above him now, crawling toward the edge. He had a gun in his right hand. When he had almost passed by, Carter sprang up like a caged tiger suddenly set loose, coming up behind the man, his left arm in a powerful grip around the man's head, his hand clamped over the man's mouth, and he drew the blade of the stiletto across the man's throat, blood suddenly gushing.

The man's gun clattered a few feet down on top of the next

lower crate. Carter waited until the body stopped twitching, and then he eased it down.

Someone was below, in the aisle. "Pete?"

Carter came to the edge, but he held back. He made the hissing sound.

"Pete?" the man below whispered.

Carter dropped over the edge, directly behind the man. The surprised man spun around wildly, and Carter drove the stiletto into his heart with his right hand while grabbing the front of his jacket with his left.

The man grunted softly, shuddered once, and slumped to the concrete floor. The odds were getting better.

Carter wiped the blade on the man's jacket sleeve, then turned and hurried back into the deeper shadows of the rear aisles. Unless he was mistaken, one more person lurked back there.

They ran into each other, literally, as Carter started around the corner.

The man was in his middle to late forties and looked as if he had worked the docks all his life. He carried a wicked-looking loading hook in his right hand.

"Christ," he swore, backing up. He swung the hook, but Carter managed to back up just out of its range.

But the longshoreman charged again. Carter stepped inside his range and clipped him neatly on the jaw with a left hook.

The man's head snapped back, and his legs started to buckle, but he recovered, swinging out with the hook and catching the sleeve of Carter's jacket, yanking him off-balance.

"Peewee! Kid!" the longshoreman shouted.

Carter feinted left, away from the hook, and then back to the right as the deadly tool missed him by an inch. He drove inward and up, the stiletto deflecting off the man's breastbone and slipping between his ribs, puncturing a lung. Carter viciously yanked the blade left, then right, opening the man's chest, blood and flecks of foam whooshing out of the cavity like air from a burst balloon.

Carter was covered with blood. He turned in a half crouch as one of the other men came around the corner with what appeared to be an Uzi in his hands.

"Jesus H. Christ," the longshoreman swore, bringing up the Israeli submachine gun.

Carter dove left into the protection of the stacks as all hell broke loose, the gun nearly deafening in the confined space. Pieces of wood tore from the crates, and bullets ricocheted off the concrete floor.

He sheathed his bloody stiletto, yanked out his Luger, and quickly scrambled to the next aisle.

The warehouse was deathly still for a long time. In the distance, outside, Carter was certain he could hear sirens. Were they coming here in response to the fight? Not unless someone had tipped them off. In any event, there wasn't much time.

"Your friends are dead," Carter called out. He peered around the edge of the stack. There was no one in the aisle. He slipped across into the next row.

"I don't want to hurt you," he called out. "I've come for Yamun."

Someone was behind him. The crates above him exploded in a fury of shots. Carter rolled right as he snapped off two shots, at least one of them hitting the longshoreman with the Uzi, who fell back against the crates and collapsed, the submachine gun clattering to the floor.

"You're next," Carter shouted angrily. The sirens were coming much closer now. There were a lot of them.

"I don't want you. I want Yamun," Carter shouted.

"I don't know no Yamun," someone shouted from near the service doors.

"Who picked up the guns from here?"

"I don't know. I don't know!" the longshoreman shouted. He was frightened; it was clear from his voice.

"I don't want a fight. I just want information," Carter said, edging closer toward the front of the building.

Something fell to the floor . . . it sounded like a gun . . . and the service door slid open, the warehouse suddenly flooding with light.

"No," Carter shouted. He jumped up, skidded around the corner into the main aisle, and raced out onto the loading docks.

There were at least a dozen police cars parked at every angle. More sirens sounded in the distance. At least two dozen cops, all of them with their guns drawn, crouched behind their cruisers, below the loading dock, and on either side of the loading doors. The longshoreman Carter had chased outside lay flat on his face in the dirt, his arms and legs spread.

"Don't move! Don't move!" one of the cops at the door shouted, nearly hysterical.

Carter stood stock-still, his Luger in clear sight. This was a very dangerous situation. Any trigger-happy cop or nervous rookie could pull the trigger, and the entire dock area would erupt.

But they had come too fast. They had arrived there within seconds of the time the shooting had begun. Someone had tipped them off. It was the only way. Which meant it was very possible that one of the officers was on Yamun's payroll, and the slightest provocation, the slightest excuse, would result in his immediate execution.

One of the policemen cautiously approached from behind Carter and snatched the Luger out of his hand.

"Son of a bitch," one of the others swore. "Look at him!"

Carter's hands were roughly pulled back, and he was handcuffed. Another officer was right behind him, the barrel of his shotgun inches from Carter's temple.

"Make one wrong move and I'll blow your brains all over the place," the shotgun-wielding officer said. He was very young and very frightened.

"He looks like a goddamned butcher," another policeman said.

"What the hell happened in there?" another one asked.

One of the police cars pulled up, and the back door was yanked open. The men on the loading dock started to lead Carter down to the car.

"I have a knife," Carter said. "You'd better take it before there's an accident."

"What?" the one with the shotgun asked.

"My right sleeve. It's there."

One of the other policemen shoved Carter's right sleeve up, and he whistled. He pulled out Hugo. "Holy . . . . Will you look at this. The blood . . ."

"Spread your legs!" one of them shouted.

Carter did as he was told, and he was frisked. They did not find the gas bomb. He decided to wait until the situation was a bit more defused before he told them about it.

They had found his wallet and his diplomatic passport, but for the moment none of the officers realized the significance of the latter.

Carter was led down to the cruiser, where he was roughly shoved into the back seat and immediately driven away.

The officer riding shotgun in the front turned around and looked at Carter.

"What the hell happened back there? You work for the mob?"

"You have my identification," Carter said.

"Yeah?"

"The passport. Look at it."

The man did. "So?"

"It's a diplomatic passport."

"You an ambassador or something? What the hell are you doing running around a warehouse in Bayonne massacring dockworkers?"

"I'll give you a number in Washington. I suggest you call it as soon as possible."

"Shit," the officer said. "You ain't in any position to suggest a goddamned thing."

They rode the rest of the way into the city of Bayonne in silence, pulling in behind the precinct house. Several cruisers had followed them from the warehouse. When they had pulled in and the officers were out, their guns drawn, Carter was led out of the car and into the building, up to the booking room.

The precinct captain came out of his office, took one look at Carter, and whistled. "Holy shit. What the hell did he get into?" He came over. "Are you injured?"

"No," Carter said.

One of the other men stepped forward. "There's at least three guys dead down in a warehouse. He . . . cut them up pretty badly."

The captain was looking at him. The officer who had ridden shotgun handed across Carter's identification and passport.

"He was mouthing off something about a diplomatic passport or something."

The captain looked at the passport, then at Carter. He knew. He nodded. "Bring him into my office."

"Sir?"

"My office, Sergeant!"

Carter was led into the man's office, and when they were alone, the captain looked hard at Carter.

"Are you involved with the U.N.? Or the CIA?"

"No, but . . ."

The captain held up his hand. "No, I don't want to know after all. I imagine you have a number in Washington for me to call. Let's get it over with."

"Right," Carter said. He gave the captain the AXE clearance number in Washington that would alert the O.D. that something was wrong. As long as he could stay there, he figured that nothing would happen to him. Yamun's connection with the precinct, probably through the mob, would not be able to get to him.

TWELVE

It was well after nine that evening before Brad Williams had come up from Washington and the proper strings had been pulled for Carter's release. The CIA, of course, knew nothing about Carter, nor did State, and the precinct captain was adamant about knowing what was going on.

Finally the director of the FBI telephoned the governor of New Jersey, who in turn called a very impressed captain, who nevertheless insisted that someone come up from Washington and personally verify that Carter was who he said he was.

After all, there were several murders attributable to the man as well as auto theft and a serious accident on a Brooklyn highway.

The captain had arranged for Carter's suitcase to be brought over from the abandoned car on the Shore Parkway. It had been towed to the impound yard, but everything inside was intact.

Carter had cleaned up and was reasonably rested by the time Williams arrived.

"Somehow I thought it might be you . . ." Carter started, but Williams seemed to be very harried and definitely worried about something.

"This your man?" the captain asked, checking Williams's

139

credentials, which showed he worked for the State Department.

"Yes, he is, Captain. And we'll request that you say nothing about this encounter."

"How about the goddamned bodies I've got cut up all over the place?"

"Put it down to prowlers, Captain."

"Prowlers," the captain repeated.

"Yes, sir."

The captain shook his head. "Get the hell out of here. You people make me sick."

Carter got up. "Thanks for your help, Captain. If you know what was actually going on, you wouldn't be so harsh. You'd be scared."

"I'm already scared. I don't need to know more," the captain said. "Now get the hell out of here, and please don't ever come back to Bayonne."

Williams held his silence until they got out to the car and left the precinct station. He headed toward the parkway going south.

"Troubles?" Carter asked. "Has Yamun already struck?"

"Troubles. Major Dunbar is back at McGuire with his B-58 waiting to take you back to Bagnolet. He says this time the meter will be running, and he'll expect a good tip."

"What is it?"

Williams looked at him. "Something very big is definitely about to happen, Nick," he said. "Nearly every goddamned Arab—not just the Libyans—has either left Washington or is preparing to leave."

"For New York?"

"Right," Williams said. "We got word this afternoon that Qaddafi is on his way over. He will talk to the U.N. at the very same moment the President speaks to Congress."

It bothered Carter. He had worried about some Libyan plot to assassinate the President during his speech. It would explain the weapons, and it would explain Yamun's involvement. But his people and the weapons were in New York, not in Washington. Whatever was going to happen was going to happen in New York, not in the capital.

"What's happened in Paris that I'm to return?" Carter asked. "I should think we'd better start working on the Libyans at the U.N."

Williams took a deep breath and let it out slowly, as if he were bracing himself.

"You're guaranteed not to like this, Nick," he said.

"What happened?"

"It's your French friend . . . Pierre Belmont. He was found shot to death this morning. We didn't hear about it until later in the day. It was a routine info-only query from the SDECE. No one connected it at first, until we realized just who it was."

"It's Yamun and his people," Carter said.

"The report indicated it seemed to be the work of the French underworld."

"La Pègre."

"Yes."

"Were any names mentioned?"

"No," Williams said. He licked his lips. "There's more."

Carter steeled himself for the worst.

"Belmont was killed at his home. His wife was murdered as well."

"What about Anita Gabrud? She was staying with them."

"She was gone. No trace of her. The Mossad is climbing all over State. They're threatening to go public unless we produce her."

"How about the SDECE? Had they known she was there?"

"Apparently not. Otherwise she would have been a chief suspect, of course, and even more hell would have broken loose."

"Thank God for small favors," Carter said absently. His mind was racing ahead. There was something missing. One factor in all of this that none of them had considered. The entire operation seemed too open for Yamun. There was something! Why had he killed Belmont? To get at Anita? If that were the case, what did Belmont have that Yamun felt was essential to his operation? Essential enough to stop what he was doing long enough to have Belmont killed. It had to be more important to Yamun at the moment than his sister's death. Only one thing could qualify: the operation itself. Belmont must have known, or at least he'd known how to get the answers.

They had crossed the bridge, and Williams headed over to the New Jersey Turnpike.

"Between the President's speech tomorrow night and Qaddafi coming, everyone is shook up. Washington is like a three-ring circus."

Still Carter was bothered. The nagging thought that he was missing something—that they *all* were—would not go away.

Qaddafi's coming to New York was simply a diversion. If that were the case, Carter reasoned, it was a diversion for what? An assassination attempt on the President? It was the ultimate terrorist threat. To kill not just any world leader, but to kill the President of the United States. In Washington.

Carter looked up. In Washington, tomorrow night while the President was speaking to the joint session of Congress. While all of America and a great portion of the world watched on television. Yamun would assassinate the President.

But the clues were in Paris. And now there were less than twenty-four hours for him to do something that the Mossad and law enforcement agencies all across Europe had been unable to do for years: find Yamun and stop him—permanently.

"As soon as you drop me off at McGuire, you're going to have to get back to Washington immediately. Tell Hawk that the President must be warned."

Williams looked over at Carter in alarm. "Warned?"

"Yamun will try to assassinate him."

"When? How?"

"I don't know how. Not yet. But the when is easy. During his speech to Congress."

"Jesus," Williams said heavily. "And there's no way to stop him from going on. You just can't cancel a State of the Union address."

"Warn him," Carter said. "Security in Washington will have to be beefed up. Only those with absolutely clear backgrounds can be let in."

"But that's impossible, Nick!" Williams said. "There are even some congressmen with questionable backgrounds. And look at the press corps!"

"I know," Carter said glumly. "I know."

Somehow Carter managed to sleep on the flight back across the Atlantic, although when he awoke as they touched down at Bagnolet outside of Paris, he almost wished he hadn't. He felt terrible.

"Am I going to have to ferry you back to New York?" Dunbar asked after they landed and had crawled out of the aircraft.

"I doubt it," Carter said, shaking the officer's hand. "Thanks for your help."

"I don't suppose you'll tell me what the hell is going on?"

Carter smiled tiredly. "I wish I knew myself. *Au revoir.*"

"*Auf wiedersehen.*"

Howard DeVries was waiting for Carter at the airport. "I was told to meet you and get you into the city, and then to do whatever you say."

Carter climbed into the CIA chief of station's car, and they started back toward Paris, his bag in the rear seat.

It was dawn. Going west he had gained hours; coming back this way he had lost. It seemed as if he had just seen the dawn over the Verrazano Narrows just a couple of hours ago. Somehow yesterday had gotten away from him. Yet so much had happened. And now there were just hours before the President was scheduled to speak before Congress. Eight o'clock that night, Washington time, in fact. It did not seem like enough time to unravel Yamun's plan, find him, and then stop him. It seemed impossible, in fact. First, however, he was going to have to find Anita Gabrud. Belmont evidently had the key. Hopefully Anita had it as well.

"I'll need a car," Carter said.

"You can have this one," DeVries said. "Anything other than that I can do to help?"

"I may need some fast air transportation."

"Back to the States again? New York?"

"No. If anywhere, Washington, D.C."

"I'll arrange something."

"Thanks," Carter said. His eyes burned and his muscles ached. It seemed as if he had not slept or eaten in months. When this was over, he promised himself a very long vacation. One in which he was going to do nothing except lie around and indulge himself.

Paris, when they came into the city, was beginning to come alive. The traffic was terrible.

DeVries pulled over on a side street a couple of blocks from the American embassy. "I get off here."

"Thanks," Carter said.

"You're sure there's nothing I can do?"

"I'm in a hurry . . ." Carter started, but DeVries was already out of the car.

"I understand," he said, and he turned and walked off. Carter watched him go. He'd have to thank him properly another time.

He slid over behind the wheel and pulled away from the curb. Anita had gotten free at Belmont's. But she had not contacted her own embassy. It meant she was still willing to work with him. She had kept her promise that she would not say anything to her own people for fear it would get back to Yamun and make an already difficult situation impossible.

She had sent him a clear signal, that she was still honoring her word. A clear signal. Carter wracked his brain. She was somewhere in Paris. She had not left the city. At least he didn't think she had. The Mossad would have spotted her through all the normal channels of escape. She was still somewhere in the city. But where?

It would have to be a place that she would be reasonably certain Carter would find her. Yet it would have to be a place that her own people, that the SDECE, and that La Pègre would not think to look.

Suddenly he knew. He hurried around the block and headed back toward the river and the bridge across the Île de la Cité to the Left Bank.

He parked the car in a back alley, then went the rest of the way on foot, the morning absolutely sparkling, lovely. He was on St. Germain-des-Prés, a lot of the early risers milling around, many of them finding company in the sidewalk cafés that were numerous in the area.

The Deux Magots wasn't far away. The café he had gone to on his first day in Paris—the one Anita had successfully followed him to—was less than a block away.

He stopped, lit a cigarette, and bought a newspaper from a sidewalk kiosk.

If she knew nothing, he would have to admit he was stumped. He'd need help. Yamun evidently was not going to rise to the bait he had given to the La Pègre boss, Paul Gide. If Anita had nothing for him, he knew he was going to have to go back to Gide. He'd kill the man if need be, but he'd find out where Yamun was and what he was planning . . . if the French hood knew.

Carter crossed the street and went the rest of the way to the café. She was there. Seated at one of the back tables, next to the wall of the building. She was alone. Drinking coffee and reading a fashion magazine. She looked beautiful.

He walked among the tables on the sidewalk and went over to her. She looked up and almost sagged with relief.

"Nick," she breathed.

He slipped into a chair across the table from her. She put out her hand and he took it. She was trembling.

"What happened at Pierre's?" he asked.

"I was in the tub. Three of them came in . . . at least I

think there were three of them. They killed your friend downstairs. Marie was up with me, getting me a clean towel, when they shot her down in the bathroom doorway.''

Alarm bells were starting to ring through Carter's system.

''They came into the bathroom, where I was . . . in the tub. They were carrying automatic weapons. One of them raised his gun and pointed it at my head. I was sure he was going to shoot.''

Carter held very still.

''Someone shouted from downstairs, and they just turned and left. Then I heard them leave, and there was the sound of a car, and then nothing. So I got dressed and got out of there, hoping you'd come back. I didn't know what else to do.''

Carter laughed out loud. He threw his head back and roared.

''N-Nick?'' she said, alarmed.

He looked at her, still laughing. ''We're being watched!'' he snapped. ''Laugh, goddammit, laugh!''

She tried to laugh, but she could not. ''What's the matter?''

Three young men crossing the street at the corner suddenly looked around, then jumped back. An instant later a Citroën DS19 roared around the corner.

''Down!'' Carter shouted, shoving the table aside. He reached out and grabbed Anita's sleeve and hauled her off her chair to the floor. As the Citroën flashed by, an intense rain of fire from at least two automatic weapons sprayed the entire café area. People were screaming, and bullets were ricocheting everywhere.

Carter had his Luger out an instant later, and he jumped to his feet and scrambled out to the street as the Citroën turned the far corner and was gone.

There was pandemonium on the street as people began picking themselves up. At least a half-dozen in the café had been hit and were down, including one of the waiters, whose head was half gone.

Anita had picked herself up. Carter raced back to her,

scooped up her purse, then grabbed her arm and propelled her out of the café and down the block as fast as their legs could carry them, the sounds of the gunfire and the screaming still ringing in their ears.

They reached the car DeVries had lent him, jumped in, and took off toward the heavier traffic of the business districts on the Right Bank.

"What happened?" Anita croaked. "How did you know?"

"They *let* you live, goddammit," Carter said angrily. He kept looking in his rearview mirror to make sure they were not being followed. Yamun had outfigured him every step of the way, including here, today.

"What happened?" Anita screeched.

"He knew Pierre had helped me. He knew you were there. So he killed Belmont but let you live."

"I don't understand, Nick . . ."

"He wants *me*, goddammit! I killed his sister. He wants to get to *me*."

"But . . ." she started, but then her eyes widened and she cut it off. "Oh, Nick! He knew! He knew that if he let me live, you'd find a way of coming to me! He had me followed. As soon as you showed up he made his move."

"Right," Carter said.

"And I know why," she said, lowering her voice.

Carter looked at her.

"It wasn't just you he wanted, Nick. It's the list."

"What list?"

"Pierre came up with a list of known Libyan activists here in Paris. Known supporters of Qaddafi . . . known supporters of his extreme measures."

"You have it?"

She nodded. "Yes, I do," she said slowly. "I've had it all along."

"Where?"

She just looked at him.

"Where is the list? Where did you hide it?"

She opened her purse and pulled out a long, narrow slip of paper. "I didn't hide it. I kept it with me."

They had come past the Louvre, and Carter pulled into one of the service entrances and parked beside a maintenance truck.

He turned in his seat and looked at Anita. "You kept it with you all this time? Do you realize what could have happened had they decided to take you?"

He took the list from her and scanned it. There were more than a dozen names and addresses, and in half the cases, businesses as well. Two of the men on the list were attorneys, evidently representing Libyan interests in the Paris and international money markets. One, intriguingly enough, was an engineer who ran his own consulting business not too far from where they were parked at that moment. Two ran galleries specializing in Middle Eastern art, and one was listed as the owner of Marchand Imports.

"Where did Pierre get this list?" Carter asked. "Did he tell you?"

"No. I presumed from his own files. From the SDECE."

"We're going to have to see these people. Today."

She nodded.

"Your people are looking for you."

"I figured as much," she said.

"Why—"

"—did I stay away?" she finished. "Why did I wait for you?"

"Yes."

"I gave you my word," she said, and when Carter started to protest she held him off. "Besides, you were right. We've been trying for Yamun for years with no luck. I thought I could give you at least a few days."

She was an amazing woman. He leaned over in the seat and kissed her. She was still trembling.

"Where did you go?" she asked when they parted. "Pierre wouldn't tell me."

"Back to the States. The weapons from the warehouse

were being shipped to New York. I followed them.''

''And?'' she asked, her eyes bright.

He told her everything that had happened, including the information Brad Williams had supplied.

''They're all leaving Washington? So when Qaddafi shows up, something will happen in New York? Is that what you're saying?''

''I think that's what Yamun wants us all to believe.''

''But?''

''Our President is speaking to a joint session of Congress tonight.''

''And you think Yamun's going to try to get in somehow and assassinate him? Qaddafi is nothing more than the diversion?''

''As are the weapons.''

She shook her head. ''The list . . .''

''Right,'' Carter said. ''Someone on Pierre's list may know something. We're going to have to find out. Immediately.''

''Then again, they may know nothing,'' Anita said.

''That's a possibility we'll worry about if and when we get to it,'' Carter said, starting the car. ''For now, we're going to go lean on some Libyans.''

''In broad daylight, with my own people gunning for me, Yamun gunning for you, and La Pègre gunning for both of us.''

''Something like that,'' he said, grinning.

THIRTEEN

Nick Carter could not get his mind off Pierre Belmont's death as he drove the few blocks from the Louvre to the first address on the list, that of an engineer, Beni Sokna. Belmont had been killed because Yamun wanted Anita to lead him to the one man he really wanted. Himself.

Ironically, Belmont had wanted to slowly back out of the business—at least the field work—get his promotion, and find a nice place in the country where he and his wife could finally relax and enjoy each other.

Belmont had been a pro. He had understood the risks they all took. Still, the thought was not comforting.

They almost missed the small sign as Carter drove slowly past the building off the rue St. Martin. Anita picked it out.

"There it is," she said. "Libyan National Engineering Consultants."

Carter continued around the block and then parked the car. At his insistence, they stayed put for a full ten minutes to make sure that Yamun or his people had not followed them there or had somehow staked out the engineer's office.

But there was nothing other than the usual traffic, and finally they got out and headed back on foot.

"Did Pierre discuss any of these people with you?" Carter asked.

"He said Sokna provided engineering help to fellow Libyans here trying to deal with French manufacturers and suppliers."

"He'd know a lot of people," Carter said.

"But he's right in the middle. His business would be jeopardized if it were too obvious that he had involved himself with terrorists."

"You're probably right, but he's a start," Carter said.

There was no one suspicious on the little street that housed a few small office supply shops, an interior decorator, and two other engineering firms.

They went inside Sokna's office, finding themselves in a tiny reception area furnished with a small desk to one side and a couple of chairs on the other. No one was seated at the desk. It was very quiet in the building.

"Hello?" Carter called out. "Mr. Sokna?"

There was no answer. They could hear a horn blaring outside from somewhere down the block, and a truck rumbled past.

This was starting to feel all wrong to Carter. He pulled out his Luger and checked to make sure there was a round in the firing chamber. Anita, alarmed, pulled out her Beretta automatic and checked to make sure it was ready to fire.

There was a door leading to the back of the building. Carter motioned for Anita to stand to one side of it while he went in. She nodded, wide-eyed, adjusting her grip on her weapon as she moved silently into place.

Carter tried the door. It was unlocked. It opened inward. He eased it open a crack, then stepped aside and shoved it the rest of the way with the toe of his shoe.

The back room smelled of electronic equipment—and something else. Something metallic that Carter instantly recognized.

"Christ," he said half to himself. He brought the Luger up, its safety off, his finger on the trigger, and spun around the doorframe and into the large back room, keeping low and moving fast, every sense alert for the slightest movement.

But he found nothing, except the odor was much stronger there.

Beni Sokna, or at least the man he took to be Sokna, was sitting in a chair in front of a small computer console, numbers flashing on the screen. He was slumped half over to the left, a small, neat hole in his right temple, only a small amount of blood on the side of his head. A woman, his secretary, lay a few feet away on the floor. She had been shot in the back of the head, her dark black hair matted and still wet with blood.

"Nick?" Anita called softly.

"They're dead," Carter said. He quickly crossed the room to the engineer and touched his neck. The body was still warm. Yamun or his people had just been there. They too, apparently, knew the list.

"My God," Anita whispered from the doorway.

"They have the list too," Carter said, spinning around. He shoved his Luger back into its shoulder holster, and he and Anita left the office at a run and raced back to their car.

He started the car, slammed it in gear, and they took off as Anita pulled out the list.

"There's a goldsmith's shop not too far from here. Just off the rue St. Antoine. I think I know the area. It's not far from the Hôtel de Ville," she said. She looked up, getting her bearings. "Turn right," she said.

Carter drove fast, weaving in and out of traffic but on the lookout for traffic police. To be stopped now would be a disaster. They were on the right track, but they were short on time . . . very short on time.

In less than five minutes they had reached the vicinity of the shop, and once again Carter parked around the corner so that they would approach on foot. They'd have a better chance that way of detecting the presence of one of Yamun's people.

"His name is Fa'id Baida," Anita said. "But Belmont

said nothing about him other than the fact that he was Libyan and was suspected of dealing in stolen goods, sending the money back to Tripoli.''

"To support terrorist activities.''

Anita shrugged. "That was the presumption.''

They rounded the corner and pulled up short. The same Citroën DS19—or its twin—that had raced past them at the café near the Deux Magots that morning was parked in front of the goldsmith's shop.

"It's them,'' Carter said. The car was empty. There was no one waiting nearby. No one seemed to be watching. Except for the presence of the car, the street seemed normal, peaceful.

"La Pègre?'' Anita asked.

"I think so,'' Carter said. He pulled out his Luger. Anita pulled out her Beretta, and holding their weapons close in to their sides so it would be less obvious to a passerby that they were armed, they approached the shop.

Carter did not think Yamun would be here now like this. Whatever it was the terrorist had planned was already in motion. He'd be somewhere in Washington by now. Getting set up, getting ready for the kill tonight. But the clues were all here, in Paris. And short of having the President cancel his State of the Union address, there was nothing else to be done except follow up with what they were learning here.

They were within ten feet of the shop when the door burst open and three men hurried out. One of them was just stuffing a pistol into his pocket.

"*Merde*,'' one of them said, reaching for his gun.

Carter fired twice, hitting him in the chest and throat, driving him backward through the front display window. At the same moment, Anita had dropped to a crouch and fired three times in rapid succession, two shots hitting the man on the far right in the chest, blood exploding out of his white shirt, driving him back onto the sidewalk. The third La Pègre assassin had his gun out and was bringing it up, when Carter fired a single shot, high, catching him in his face, just below his right eye. His head snapped back, and he collapsed on top of the man who had crashed through the window.

Someone was shouting something, and a woman was screaming.

Carter and Anita turned around and walked back around the corner to their car without a word.

Before any sirens sounded they were several blocks away, driving at a normal speed so as not to attract any attention.

Now that they had struck back, Anita was much calmer. Carter lit a cigarette. She took it from him, and he lit himself another.

"Who is next on the list?" he asked.

"Why is he doing this, Nick? Why is he killing his own people?"

Carter glanced at her. "They either knew or suspected too much. This operation is too important to him to risk having it exposed. He'll kill them all . . . to keep them silent."

"Even his friends, his helpers?"

"He's a dedicated man."

She shuddered, but she looked at the list. "U'Lam Murzuk. He is an attorney. His office is across from the Banque de France near the Palais Royal."

They were up near the Porte St.-Denis. In less than five minutes they were back in the vicinity of the Comédie Française, and Carter parked the car.

"If he only sent out one team, we may be in luck," Carter said as they started around the corner on foot.

It was getting to be late morning. He was very conscious that time was very short for them. There would have to be some point at which he would have to cut off their investigations here in Paris and take the flight that DeVries promised he'd set up. If it came down to the last minute, they'd have to operate in Washington around the President himself.

The day was very warm and pleasant. There were a lot of tourists out and about, and the traffic was very heavy.

They crossed the narrow street in front of the Banque de France and entered the office building where Murzuk's office was located.

"Belmont figured he was one of the main finance men for Qaddafi's European operations," Anita said.

"Why haven't the French sent him packing?"

"His presence here was apparently too profitable. And technically he apparently wasn't doing anything illegal, at least nothing against French law."

The attorney's office was listed on the fourth floor. They took the marble stairs up.

His name was lettered in gold on a frosted glass door. Carter listened a moment, but he could hear nothing. Anita reached into her purse as he opened the door, and they went inside.

A pretty young woman was seated behind a huge desk in a reception office. The door to Murzuk's office was open behind her. They could see the dark, slightly built attorney hurriedly stuffing papers into two fat briefcases.

The secretary reached for the telephone, but Anita had her gun out and motioned for the woman to put the phone down.

Carter was across the office in three steps, his Luger out. Murzuk looked up and scrambled on his desk for his gun.

"Pick it up and you're dead, *monsieur*," Carter snapped in French.

The attorney's hand hesitated over the weapon. His complexion had gone pale. He looked as if he would collapse at any moment.

"Some of your friends are already dead. Yamun sent his people around to kill them. Is that why you're leaving?"

Murzuk shook his head. "Please . . . please," he cried.

"I'm not here to hurt you," Carter said. "I want Yamun."

"I don't know any person of that name . . ."

Carter was across the office in a second. He shoved the attorney's gun away and laid the muzzle of the Luger against the man's cheek.

"I'm not here to hurt you if you cooperate. If not, we'll

just wait to see which one of Yamun's people shows up.''

The attorney was trembling. "If I . . . cooperate . . ."

"They you get to walk out of here alive."

The man laughed, the sound anything but a response to humor. "I am a dead man no matter what."

"Not if I can get to Yamun first and kill him," Carter said. Something came into the attorney's eyes. A cunning.

"How do I know—"

Carter cut him off savagely. "I want him! Now!"

"I know nothing . . . I swear it . . ."

"Then you're a dead man," Carter said.

"No!" his secretary screamed.

Murzuk's eyes went even wider. Carter could see he wanted to go to the woman.

"Anita," Carter called out.

"Yes?"

"I want you to shoot the woman in ten seconds."

The secretary let out a little cry.

"You can't be serious," the attorney said. He was getting very desperate.

"I want Yamun. I'll do anything to get to him."

"Five," Anita said. "Six . . ."

"No . . . No!" the attorney cried.

"Yamun," Carter pressed.

"Seven . . . eight . . ."

"I'll tell you! I'll tell you!"

"Hold it a minute," Carter called to Anita.

The attorney looked from the doorway to Carter and back.

"Yamun," Carter said.

"I don't know the details," the man started, but Carter shoved him back with the muzzle of the Luger.

"Yamun!"

"It has to do with London," the attorney said at last.

"London? Not Washington?"

"No . . . no, I know nothing about Washington. It is to be London."

London? Carter didn't know if he could believe the man.

Yet the attorney was certain his life and the life of his secretary, whom he apparently loved, were in jeopardy. But London, and not Washington?

"When is this supposed to take place?"

"I don't know. Sometime tonight. Around ten o'clock."

"What is it he's going to do in London at ten this evening?" Carter demanded.

"I don't know. I swear to Allah, I do not know. I have told you everything. And now my life is forfeit."

Ten o'clock tonight in London? Had Yamun outmaneuvered him again? Carter wondered. Qaddafi was speaking in New York, and weapons had been shipped to New York. Both red herrings? The President was speaking at eight o'clock tonight, Washington time, which made it about one in the morning here. The Libyans had been streaming out of the city. Was that still another red herring? Were they all shams to divert attention from some real operation that would take place tonight in London?

But ten o'clock. Where was the significance? What was he missing?

"Is he alone?"

"He is never alone," the attorney said.

"He has other people helping him?"

"I don't know."

"How did you know about tonight? About London?" Carter asked.

The attorney backed up toward the big window that faced the street. He started to say something, when the window shattered and he was thrown violently forward, the top of his skull spraying over his desk.

Carter dove to the right.

The secretary screamed and burst into the office. For a split second she stopped, seeing Murzuk's shattered body. She screamed again, raced past Carter, and leaped for the window.

"No!" Carter shouted, but it was too late.

The woman hurled herself through the broken glass, cutting her face, arms, and legs to ribbons, and then she was gone, falling four stories to the pavement below.

"My God . . . my God . . ." Anita kept saying over and over again.

There was no time to hang around. Carter grabbed Anita's arm and spun her around, and together they raced out of the office and into the broad corridor. There were several people in the hall who had stepped out of their offices because of the commotion. Carter was covered with Murzuk's blood, and he and Anita both held their weapons in plain sight. Everyone scattered.

They ran down the corridor and started down the stairs. The police would be on their way by now. And whoever had shot and killed Murzuk had been waiting outside for the attorney to appear at the window. They had not come up because they knew Carter and Anita were there.

On the second floor, instead of continuing down, Carter shoved Anita out into the corridor, and they burst into the first door on the left. The legend on the glass indicated it was the office of a financial consultant.

Two men in business suits stood talking. An older woman sat behind the reception desk. There didn't appear to be anyone in the inner office.

They all looked up, their eyes going wide.

"Get out of here!" Carter yelled in French, waving his gun around like a wild man. "Move!"

They all stumbled out the door, and when they were gone, Carter went to the phone on the desk. "Lock the door," he said to Anita.

He picked up the phone and dialed the number for the American embassy. It seemed to ring forever.

Outside were the sounds of a lot of sirens. People were shouting, and someone was screaming something.

"Connect me with Howard DeVries!" Carter shouted. "This is an emergency!"

"One moment, please, sir," the embassy operator said with maddening deliberateness.

There was a commotion in the corridor. Anita turned around. "Someone is coming, Nick!" she said.

"Come on," Carter said into the phone.

DeVries was on. "Hello?"

"This is Carter."

"Carter, where the hell are you? The Mossad is here looking for blood."

"Listen to me, Howard, and listen carefully. Anita Gabrud and I are in the office building just across from the Banque de France near the Palais Royale. On the second floor."

"I know the building."

"The police are here. They think we are murderers. La Pègre, under the direction of the Libyan terrorist Yamun, have killed a number of people, including a Libyan attorney here in this building. We must get out of here."

"I'll be right there, although I don't know how much I'll be able to do. Half of Paris is after you."

"Call the SDECE. I was a friend of Pierre Belmont. My assignment has something to do with his murder. But move, we're running out of time!"

"On my way, Nick," DeVries said, and he hung up.

Carter put down the phone. Anita had backed away from the door. There were a lot of people in the corridor.

"We know you are in there," an amplified voice boomed from the hallway.

Carter motioned for Anita to come back with him to the inner office.

"You have sixty seconds to lay down your weapons, and then lie flat on the floor with your faces down," the voice boomed.

Carter and Anita went into the inner office and silently closed the heavy wooden door. He pulled a chair around and propped it up under the doorknob.

"When we come in, we will fire on any movement. You now have fifty-five seconds."

"Someone is coming to help," Carter said. He made a

wide circle around to the window, then carefully looked down at the street. It was filled with French police cars, uniformed officers, and hundreds of spectators being kept back beyond the corner.

"Will your friend make it on time?" Anita asked fearfully.

"I don't know," Carter said.

"Thirty seconds," the amplified voice in the corridor boomed.

"Put your gun on the desk," Carter said. He put down his Luger.

She did the same, and they got down on the floor in plain sight, to wait.

"What happened up there? What did he tell you?" Anita asked. "I couldn't hear a thing. But suddenly he was dead."

"Someone outside saw him from the window and fired. It had to have been a high-powered rifle. They knew we were here."

"If he's penetrated Aman or the Mossad, then I'll bet anything he's gotten to the gendarmes," she said.

"It's the chance we're going to have to take. But I'm not going to fire on innocent cops. No matter what," Carter said.

"But what did Murzuk tell you? What's going on? Is Yamun in Washington after the President?"

"I don't know," Carter said. "He said something about London . . . tonight . . ."

There was a burst of gunfire, and the outer door crashed open. There was a lot of shouting, and more gunfire split the heavy oak inner door, the bullets shattering the windows behind them.

"Down!" Carter shouted.

FOURTEEN

The sun was shining brightly, and there were a lot of people crowded around as the ambulance attendants brought out two gurneys, each bearing a body covered by a sheet.

The crowd moved back as the wheeled stretchers were hurried across the broad sidewalk and into two ambulances standing by.

Howard DeVries, the CIA chief of station for Paris, emerged from the building moments later with Claude Levant of the SDECE and Henri Folletee of the Paris police. They watched as the ambulances were closed up and then departed. DeVries shook his head, and then the three of them climbed into the back of a big, black Citroën Chapron limousine and they left.

Gradually the crowd cleared, and two more ambulances appeared to take away the bodies of the Libyan attorney and his secretary.

The sheet was pulled away, and Nick Carter sat up. He grinned. "I was never so happy to see anyone in my life," he said.

Howard DeVries helped him down from his gurney, and Henri Follette helped Anita down from hers. She was still shaking.

They were in the basement of the city morgue. Follette did

163

not seem particularly happy, but Levant, the SDECE man, was fuming.

"You owe us an explanation, *monsieur*, that goes far beyond what *Monsieur* DeVries has told us," Levant said.

"You'll get it, sir. But we're going to need your cooperation," Carter said.

They went down the corridor and into an elevator that brought them up to the large offices of the coroner. No one was there. Follette poured them all a stiff measure of cognac. When they had finished their drinks, Carter lit a cigarette for himself and for Anita.

"It is Abd-el Yamun," Carter began.

"The mad dog," Levant mused. "So that's why the Mossad is on the rampage."

"He was here in Paris, I believe. And we had him cornered—or we thought we did—in Aubervilliers."

"The farmhouse," Follette, the Paris police chief, said.

"Yes. My friend Pierre Belmont arranged to have me out there. But we missed him."

"It is the only reason I agreed to help you, *monsieur*. Your actions out there saved a lot of lives."

Carter inclined his head.

"But poor Belmont was ultimately not so fortunate for his association with you," Levant, the SDECE man, snapped.

"You can't know how sorry I am," Carter said. "But there is no time for this. Yamun is getting set to strike again. And this time it will be big."

"Where and when?" DeVries asked. "Here in Paris?"

"No," Carter said. He glanced at Anita. "We're going to have to keep the Mossad out of this, at least for the moment."

Levant nodded. "There is no one except us in this room who know you two survived. You can thank Howard for that."

"Let's keep it that way for now."

Levant nodded. "That will depend entirely upon your explanation. You might as well begin with just who you are. Howard tells us you are not CIA."

"No, I'm not."

"Who do you work for?"

"I'm after Yamun, and we're going to have to leave it at that."

"That's not good enough—" Levant began, but DeVries cut him off.

"Let's leave it, Claude. Later, if you need an explanation, I'm sure something can be worked out."

Levant was clearly not pleased, but he nodded.

"Yamun, as I said, is getting set for something very big," Carter began. He quickly explained what he had come up with so far, including the business with the arms shipment to the U.S., and Qaddafi's planned speech in New York, as well as Carter's earlier theory that Yamun was planning to assassinate the President during his televised State of the Union address.

"Which is scheduled for eight tonight, Washington time," DeVries said.

"That's right. And all the Libyans have left Washington. But Murzuk told me that whatever Yamun was planning would take place tonight. In London."

"Where and when?" Follette asked.

"Ten o'clock. But I don't know where—and I don't even know what," Carter said.

"Is this Murzuk's information reliable?" DeVries asked.

"I had a gun to his head, and Anita was gettimg set to pull the trigger on his secretary, for whom he apparently had a great feeling."

"It was mutual," Anita added. "My God, she jumped out the window after he was killed."

"Is there anything on the gunman outside?" Carter asked.

"No one saw a thing," Follette said, shaking his head.

"You're sure it has nothing to do with Washington?" DeVries asked. He was clearly worried about Carter's speculation that Yamun was planning to kill the President.

"No, I'm not," Carter admitted. "But at this point I don't know what to think, for sure. Murzuk was telling me the truth

. . . as far as he knew it. And he was killed to prevent him from telling me, which lends even more credence to it. What about the others on the list?''

"One of them, another attorney, is dead,'' Follette said. "I have not yet heard about the others, but I suspect we are already too late.''

DeVries looked at his watch. ''It's just a couple of minutes after twelve. Gives us less than ten hours,'' he said. ''What do you want to do, Nick?''

"Go to London. The President is being warned.''

"He won't cancel his speech.''

"No, of course not. But he has been warned. Security will be beefed up.''

"If Yamun has a mind of somehow getting to your president and assassinating him, mere security measures will not stop him,'' Levant said.

Again the same haunting feeling that he was missing something came over Carter. Yamun was simply too sharp to do anything so simple. There was a connection between London at ten o'clock tonight and the President's speech, which was scheduled to begin at eight that evening, Washington time.

Ten o'clock London time was the same as five in the afternoon in Washington, three hours before the President was scheduled to step up to the podium in front of the joint session of Congress, in front of the television cameras.

Three hours' time difference. It did not make sense.

"You'll need transportation across the Channel,'' Levant was saying. ''But it will complicate things somewhat if Miss Gabrud comes along. The Mossad wants her body. They are bringing a lot of political pressure to bear on my government.''

"She's coming along. We'll have to work out something, but from this point on we're going to remain dead. All we need is another ten hours.''

DeVries nodded.

"One way or the other it'll be over by then.''

"I'm afraid so," DeVries said. "I'll contact Thompson in London. He can set up that end of it for you. Meanwhile, I'll see what I can do to hold the Mossad off. Perhaps your bodies were stolen by Yamun's people."

"We will arrange to get you out of here and out to Orly. There will be a helicopter to Heathrow," Levant said. "We will have you there by one-thirty." He picked up the telephone and dialed a number.

Carter turned to Follette. "One thing here in Paris. A man named Paul Gide, the head of a La Pègre faction, should be picked up."

The police chief looked startled. "Gide? How does he figure in this business?"

"He runs Marchand Imports. They were the ones who transshipped the guns to New York. Some of his people were at Aubervilliers."

"He was found shot to death an hour ago," Follette said. "It was on my radio."

It was the one unexpected piece of news, and it nearly rocked Carter back on his heels.

"Nick?" Anita asked uncertainly.

"What is it, *monsieur*?" Levant asked, looking up from the phone.

Everyone who knew anything about Yamun's plans, all the weak links, had been eliminated. But Gide was a part of the power structure. He had sent weapons—at a risk to his own business—to New York for Yamun. To repay the La Pègre chief by killing him meant that Yamun was burning his bridges. It could only mean that whatever Yamun was planning for tonight was so big—and so stunning—that it would not matter who had helped it. It could even be his last act. A suicide mission? Carter wondered.

"If Gide is dead, Yamun did it," Carter said.

"He's here? In Paris?" Anita asked, her eyes bright.

"Not anymore. He'll be in London by now. But it means he's not coming back here, and it also means that he's still on this side of the Atlantic."

"Washington is definitely out, then?" DeVries asked.

"I don't know. But Yamun is in London now. I know it!"

Carter was given fresh clothes—English tweeds—his hair was dyed with gray streaks, and his face was made up, aging him by at least fifteen years. No one thing had been done to drastically alter his appearance, but taken as a whole, the change was startling.

Anita was given flashy clothes and a blond wig, along with pale blue contact lenses.

Carter was a British professor, and Anita was a European movie actress.

No one paid them the slightest attention as they took a cab out to Orly Airport, and from there took the regularly scheduled cross-Channel helicopter shuttle to London's Heathrow Airport.

Yamun had already proven his resilience and resourcefulness, and he had definitely shown just how important this project was. Carter did not think the changes in their appearances would completely fool him, but it would make it easier for them to get closer to him. From that point on it would be up to Carter. Either Yamun was the better man, or Carter was. And for the first time in his career, N3 was not one hundred percent sure of the answer to that.

There were only a few puffy white clouds over the Channel during their crossing, and moments after they had touched down at Heathrow Airport, the majestic Concorde supersonic aircraft, its futuristic nose drooping, swooped in for a landing.

They were met at the helicopter by two British Secret Intelligence Service legmen, and were led immediately across the tarmac and into the administration building.

The elevator dropped them off on the fourth floor, and they were escorted to the airport administrator's office. Their bags would be brought up later.

"Nick Carter, is it?" a tall, distinguished-looking man

said, coming across the office when they came in. There were two other men there.

"Yes," Carter said, shaking his hand. "This is Anita Gabrud, Mossad."

"Pleased to meet you both," the man said. "I'm Geoffrey Thompson, chief of Station for the Company here in London. And I don't mind telling you that DeVries's call was most disturbing."

"We're not going to have a lot of time. There is a lot of ground to cover," Carter said. He wasn't very hopeful.

"I've brought along reinforcements," Thompson said. He introduced the other two men. "Sir Thomas Doyle, chief of SIS domestic operations. And Bronson Wyckoff, Scotland Yard."

They all shook hands. Doyle was very tall and lanky, with a pink complexion and snow white hair. Bronson, on the other hand, was built like a Sherman tank, with a thick head of dark brown hair and deep, intensely dark eyes. He looked like a caricature of a Russian.

When they were all settled at a conference table in the outer office, Thompson poured them some coffee.

"DeVries didn't tell me much, except that you are here on the highest of priorities—which, naturally, I verified—and that you are shagging after Abd-el Yamun."

"The mad dog is loose again?" Doyle said, leaning forward. Evidently Thompson had not completely briefed them.

"Yes, he is," Carter said. "Did DeVries tell you anything else?" he asked Thompson.

"Just that you and Miss Gabrud had had some trouble in Paris, and that the Mossad was to be temporarily locked out of this one. Which is why you are here in mufti, so to speak."

Carter glanced at Anita. She was worn out but clearly determined to continue.

"Yamun is not only out, he has managed to kill a number of people in Paris and arrange for the deaths of a number of others in Aubervilliers and in Bayonne, New Jersey."

Thompson's eyebrows rose. "An odd combination," he said. "What is Yamun up to, then?"

"We don't know for sure," Carter said. "He was spotted outside of Tripoli and again—by me—in Beirut. It was my opinion that he was coming out to do something big. Something very big."

"Any ideas?" Wyckoff asked.

"I was convinced that he was going to Washington, D.C., to assassinate the President, who speaks this evening at a joint session of Congress."

"Good God," Thompson breathed. "You *did* use the past tense."

"I got it in Paris—from a man I consider to be a reliable source—that whatever it was Yamun was up to, whatever big thing he was planning, would apparently take place tonight around ten o'clock."

"In Washington?"

"No. Here in London."

"That tears it," Wyckoff said.

"What exactly is it he has planned, Mr. Carter? Any ideas?" Doyle asked.

"No," Carter said. "Just that it'll be very big."

"Well, how about this reliable source of yours? Can we lean on him for more information?" Wyckoff asked. He looked angry. Carter didn't think he'd want to go up against him. He looked strong as an ox.

"He's dead," Carter said. He leaned forward. "We don't have a lot of time, around eight hours, to stop whatever it is Yamun has up his sleeve. I've been up against him once, and he's danced around me several times already, so I can tell you that he's very good. But right now I believe he is desperate. He's killed everyone who has helped him to this point."

"Sounds like his last big deal," Doyle said.

"That's what I thought," Carter said. "We're going to have to work together."

"We'll turn London upside down, if need be, and smoke the bloody bastard out," Wyckoff growled.

"I don't think it's going to be quite that easy," Carter said.

"Well, we're not going to sit around here doing nothing . . ." the Scotland Yard chief snapped.

In ten minutes Carter gave them as much background on Yamun as he knew, including the business in Beirut, the fight at the Aubervilliers farmhouse, the business in Bayonne, and the murders of the Libyans in Paris.

"There's an office of Marchand Imports here in London," Wyckoff said. "We've had them under a loose watch for some time now. They have connections with this La Pègre leader of yours."

"That's a start," Carter said. "Although I think it may be a ruse."

"If Yamun's going to need weapons for whatever he's doing here in London, he might have gotten them through La Pègre. Why not? The connections were already in place. And we haven't watched them that closely."

"I can come up with a list of known Libyan sympathizers still left in London," Doyle said.

"They'll have to be checked, one at a time," Carter said. "But quietly. I don't want Yamun warned that we're on to him here. And I especially don't want him to know that Miss Gabrud and I survived."

"I'll get the ball rolling now," Doyle said. He got up and went to the other office to use the telephone.

Thompson was staring at Carter. Wyckoff picked it up. "What is it?" the Scotland Yard investigator asked.

"There's more, isn't there," Thompson said.

Carter nodded. "There was too much going on back in the States. The President is a tempting target."

"But you say Yamun's here in London," Thompson said.

"He was in Paris hours ago. He must still be on this side of the Atlantic. He could not have gotten across to the States that fast. And the man we questioned was certain it was going to happen here in London tonight at ten o'clock."

"But?" Thompson prompted. "You have a hunch?"

"A strong one. But I can't ignore the facts."

Wyckoff got to his feet. "I don't mind telling you that this makes me very nervous, Mr. Carter," he said. He looked at Thompson. "I would suggest you cull through your files at the embassy to see what you can come up with. We need some sort of a Libyan connection here. Someone who can tell us what's happening."

Thompson got up. He was upset. "I don't know if there's anything else I can do," he said.

"Miss Gabrud and I will remain here," Carter said. "As soon as you hear anything—no matter how slight—I want to know. If you get him cornered, don't try to take him. I don't care how many people you've got."

"He can't be that good," Wyckoff protested.

"A lot of your people will end up dead if you push him."

"You're the specialist?" the Scotland Yard man asked.

"In a way," Carter replied.

Wyckoff was going to make a reply, but something in Carter's eyes kept him quiet. He glanced at Thompson, then turned on his heel and left.

Doyle came back. "I'll go into town. We'll have a team at the Marchand Imports warehouse within the hour."

"Be careful . . ." Carter started, but Doyle held him off.

"I heard," he said. He turned and left.

Thompson was still staring at Carter. "It won't be here in London, will it?"

Carter shook his head slowly. "I just don't know. Maybe you should look for a Libyan Air Force connection here. Some way for Yamun to get back to Washington yet this afternoon or tonight in time for the President's speech."

"Will do," Thompson said. "I'll call Washington. We'll have to make sure that Yamun hasn't already come in. He might be on one of the flights."

"Perhaps," Carter said.

"Someone from the airport administrator's office will be in to see to your needs. If it's going to happen tonight, I'd suggest you both get something to eat and get some rest." Thompson shook hands, then he turned and left.

Anita looked at Carter. "He's right, isn't he? About it not being here in London?"

"I don't know."

"Are you afraid of losing him?" she asked harshly. "Or are you more afraid for your president?"

Carter went across to the windows and looked out across the airport. Had this become an ego trip for him? Yamun was very good. One of the best he had ever come up against. Was he merely trying to win the contest, angry that someone had bested him? Was he trying to prove to himself, and to David Hawk, that he was still the best?

FIFTEEN

A blanket of law enforcement settled on the city of London as the afternoon deepened into early evening, but still there were no signs that Yamun was there, or ever had been.

There was nothing at Marchand Imports other than the routine goods found in any import warehouse.

Wyckoff's people leaned on at least two dozen known Libyan sympathizers, and leaned on them hard. But no one knew a thing. Unlike Paris, in London Yamun apparently worked alone.

At Heathrow Airport, security had gone through lists of arriving passengers for the past few days, looking for a name or series of names that might trigger some memory, some record, that Yamun could have slipped into the country under cover. But again they came up with nothing.

For the most part, Nick Carter and Anita Gabrud remained in the airport administrator's suite of offices. They had had something to eat, but neither of them had been able to get any rest.

The incoming calls were steady but negative, and everyone was getting desperate.

At one point, Thompson asked if Carter wanted transportation arranged to the States. He promised he could get Carter back before the President's speech began. But Carter declined. It was here. In London. He could feel Yamun's presence.

It was nearly nine London time—still only four in the afternoon in Washington—when Carter hung up the phone after talking with Brad Williams in Washington.

Everything that could be done to beef up security around the President had been done. Every precaution within the city had been taken. There was nothing else they could do.

Carter checked his Luger, then stuffed it back into his holster. Anita was watching him.

"It's getting close," she said.

He could feel something. Yamun was there. He just knew it. "Let's go," he said quietly.

She jumped up. "Where?"

"For a walk."

He strode through the outer office, Anita right behind him. The room had been set up as a communications center; several people from the Yard, from the SIS, and from the American embassy were there. They looked up in alarm as Carter and Anita passed, then got on the phones. Not one of them had the authority to stop Carter.

Carter and Anita took the elevator down to the ground floor, and then took the broad, main-level corridor across to the international terminal.

It was a long way, and as Carter walked, Anita at his side, something kept hammering at the back of his head. He knew, goddammit, he knew! Yamun was in London, but it would happen in Washington. But *what* would happen in Washington?

They stepped onto one of the moving walkways and held onto the rail. The further into the terminal and baggage area they went, the more people there were. The big airport, one of the busiest in the world, never slept. The shops and bars were open twenty-four hours a day. There were always people coming and going. Always in a hurry.

Inside the terminal Carter stopped. He looked around. Yamun was there. At Heathrow. Somehow he knew it. He did not believe in ESP, but he was a believer in his own hunches that came about through a subconscious juggling of the facts he already knew.

He looked at his watch. It was already well after nine. Less than a half hour until ten.

They had gone across the terminal and had started up to the observation platform, when the public address system blared. First in French and then in English, a voice announced the boarding of the Concorde SST to Washington, D.C. It was scheduled for departure at 2200 hours. Ten o'clock.

Carter stopped in his tracks, the impact almost physical. He spun around.

"Nick?" Anita said in alarm.

People near them looked at his face then stepped around him.

London! Ten o'clock! It took the Concorde three and a half hours to reach Washington from London. In three and a half hours it would be just 8:30 P.M., Washington time. The President would just be getting started with his speech. He'd speak for at least an hour. Time enough for Yamun to make it from the airport. Time enough for him to do whatever it was he had planned.

"The Concorde!" he shouted, and he grabbed Anita and headed toward its gate at a dead run.

The uniformed security people all looked up in alarm as Anita and Carter came around the corner and skidded to a halt.

"Call the administrator's office immediately!" Carter shouted. He looked beyond the electronic security gate, and down the hall toward the VIP lounge that served the Concorde. The corridor was empty. Everyone ready to board the plane was already there.

The security people were just looking at Carter.

"For God's sake, man, call the administrator's office! My name is Carter. I'm a cop, and I've got to get aboard the Concorde."

"Now, sir, if you'll just show us your identification," one of the security officers said.

"Right," Carter said, half turning away. He reached inside his jacket, pulled out Wilhelmina, and turned back.

"Bloody hell!" the guard swore. He and the others stepped back.

"Final boarding call for Concorde SST service to Washington and Miami. All passengers should be in place at this time. Final boarding call . . ."

Carter yanked back the Luger's ejector slide. "Now! Call now!" he shouted urgently.

The guard picked up the wall phone and dialed the number. It was answered a moment later.

"This is Albright on the SST gate. I've got a man with a gun here, claims he's a cop," he said. His eyes widened. He held out the phone.

Carter stepped in and grabbed it. He holstered his Luger. One of Wyckoff's people was on the line.

"This is Carter, and I want you to listen very carefully," Carter said.

The guard had stepped back and had pulled out his gun. The other two guards did the same.

"Go ahead, sir."

"He's aboard the Concorde ready to take off right now for Washington."

"Christ," the officer swore. "We can stop the plane . . ."

"No!" Carter shouted. "He'd just hold the passengers hostage. And we don't know yet what he's got planned for Washington."

"What do you want to do, sir?"

"I have to get aboard. Miss Gabrud will come with me. We'll let the flight leave as scheduled. On the way over we'll find out what he has planned."

"I don't know . . ."

"Alert Washington. They can be standing by to grab him when he gets off. But I've got four nervous security guards all pointing guns at me and not very long to get aboard. They've already loaded.''

Wyckoff's man hesitated for just a moment. ''Put Albright on.''

Carted stepped back and held out the phone. ''Albright! He wants to speak to you, and you'd better hurry. Lives depend on it.''

The security guard approached cautiously, his gun still up. He took the phone, listened for a full minute, then said, ''Yes, sir.'' He hung up the phone and put his gun away. ''Stand down, boys, this one's for real.''

''The passengers who came through here. Were there any Arabs?''

The guard nodded. ''A couple of woman and at least three men.''

''That's it,'' Carter said to Anita.

''They said they'd call the boarding gate in the VIP lounge for you, sir,'' the guard said, but Carter and Anita had pushed through the electronic screening device, the machine beeping like crazy, and were racing down the corridor to the VIP lounge.

There was no way for Yamun or his people to get to the checked-on luggage in the hold of the aircraft, and they had evidently not triggered the security measures here at the gate. If they had weapons, they'd have to be unusual.

They pulled up short at the door to the VIP lounge and boarding gate area, and Carter cautiously peered through the window.

The door to the boarding tunnel was still open. A uniformed flight attendant stood by the door. A uniformed woman stood behind the desk. She had just picked up the telephone and was talking with someone. There was no one else in the modernistic lounge except for the bartender at the far side. Everyone was aboard the SST.

Carter opened the door, and he and Anita slipped inside. The man at the door started forward.

''Sir . . . ?'' he began.

But the woman on the phone held up her hand for him to stop. She was looking at Carter. She nodded. ''Yes, sir, I understand,'' she said into the phone, and then she hung up. ''Mr. Carter?'' she asked.

Carter and Anita came across to the desk. He nodded.

''Everyone is aboard, sir. There are a pair of seats at the rear of the aircraft.'' She made out two boarding passes, then handed them across. She turned to the man by the door. ''Take them aboard, Larry.''

''But quietly,'' Carter said. ''We're just ordinary passengers. And don't use my name.''

''Yes, sir,'' the attendant said uncertainly. He turned and went down the boarding tunnel, Carter and Anita right behind him.

They came around a sharp bend in the tunnel, then stepped aboard the aircraft. Their seats were at the back, which meant they'd have to walk right by a suspicious, nervous Yamun.

Carter surreptitiously slipped his Luger from its holster and shoved the weapon into his jacket pocket. He kept his finger on the trigger.

A flight attendant took their boarding passes and motioned them toward the rear. ''If you'll just find your seats and strap in, we'll be taxiing for takeoff shortly,'' she said with a pretty smile.

The aircraft was nearly full. Carter started down the aisle, Anita right behind him.

He spotted Yamun four seats back. He was seated with a young, hard-looking Arab woman. Two rows behind him, but on the opposite side of the aisle, were another Arab couple. And a half-dozen seats behind them was a third Arab man.

Yamun looked up, directly at Carter, his eyes penetrating. Carter's grip tightened on the Luger. He smiled and nodded. Yamun lowered his eyes and looked away, and Carter and Anita passed, and found their seats. Anita sat at the window, Carter on the aisle.

Seconds later the doors were shut and the cabin pressurized; Carter could feel it in his ears. The SST's gigantic engines whined into life, the lights blinking, and a couple of minutes later they were jerked backward, swung around by the tractor, and then they headed out toward the runway.

"Good evening, ladies and gentlemen," the captain's voice said. "Welcome to British Airways Supersonic Transport service to Washington. We'll be flying at approximately seventy thousand feet at a speed of fourteen hundred miles per hour. That's twice the speed of sound. We call it Mach two. On the center and forward bulkheads there is an indicator that will tell you our speed."

They turned off the taxiway and pulled up just before the end of the runway.

The captain came back on the intercom.

"Our flying time to Washington will be three hours and twenty minutes, putting us there at eight-twenty this evening." He chuckled. A few passengers laughed. "That's right. We'll arrive in Washington an hour and a half before we took off."

The engines were tested, and finally they turned onto the end of the runway, the plane swinging around, the engines coming up to power even before they were all the way around, and then they were accelerating down the runway, the G-forces gently pressing them back in their seats.

The Concorde rotated, and with a final bump they were airborne, the angle of ascent steepening as they gained speed, the landing gear grinding up into the body of the airplane, London receding below and behind them.

It would be very close for Yamun, Carter figured. If they actually touched down in Washington at 8:20, there'd have to be a car waiting for them to get them into the city before the President's speech was over. Traffic, breakdowns, or a delay in landing would all scratch the plan. Carter was uncomfortable with that line of thinking. Yamun was a man who left nothing to chance.

They continued to climb, but after a few minutes the angle leveled out, and the Mach indicator over the bulkhead blinked on, showing them passing Mach .72.

Carter was so close. He had finally come face-to-face with Yamun, and still he wasn't sure what the man was up to. And how he was going to pull it off. But Carter knew that he was still missing one of the pieces. His brain was racing.

He had seen five Arabs aboard. Three men and two women. It didn't balance. The security guard had said at least three men. . . .

"Oh, shit," Carter muttered, turning. Anita's eyes went wide.

The barrel of an oddly shaped gun was pressed into the side of Carter's head. A fourth Arab man was seated behind them.

"We wondered if you would make the flight, Mr. Carter," the Arab said. "You and your Jewess slut are welcome to die with us." He laughed.

The rest of it came to Carter in a blinding flash. And he suddenly felt very stupid for not having figured it out before.

They weren't planning on landing in Washington. They were not going to approach the Capitol, somehow try to get in past security, and then take a potshot at the President. It was much simpler, and far more deadly than that.

Yamun had a pilot with him. They were going to take over control of the Concorde and crash it into the Capitol building itself. At Mach 2. While the President was speaking.

The Concorde would become one huge guided missile, her three-quarters-empty fuel tanks like huge, deadly charges, and the pure speed of impact would wipe out not only the building and everyone—absolutely everyone—in it, but would probably break every window in the city.

The President, Vice-President, speaker of the house, all the senators and congressmen, the cabinet, the Joint Chiefs of Staff, every important government leader would be there. All of them killed in one tremendous explosion.

The missile defense system that ringed Washington was on the lookout for foreign planes. For unidentified aircraft. But the Concorde was expected. By the time air defense realized the SST was coming in far too fast, it would be too late to launch their ground-to-air missiles.

Yamun and the other four toward the front of the aircraft suddenly got out of their seats and went forward.

Carter started to get up, but the Arab pressed the muzzle of his gun against his temple.

"I don't want to kill you . . . not like this," he said.

There was a small thump forward, and the door to the flight deck popped open.

Someone shouted something, and suddenly a woman screamed up front.

The Arab behind Carter was grinning. "It has begun . . ." he started to say.

All his attention had been on Carter. Anita had managed to open her purse. She pulled out the Beretta automatic, and firing through the back of her seat, she squeezed off two shots.

The Arab was flung backward against his seat at the same instant that the Mach indicator on the forward bulkhead chimed and went to 1.1 as they passed the speed of sound at well over seven hundred miles per hour.

The sound of Anita's gun was muffled by the seat back and ignored in the general pandemonium that had enveloped the aircraft.

Carter tore off his seat belt. The time for action was right then, before order was restored by Yamun's people. But he could not use his Luger for fear of a stray shot puncturing the hull of the aircraft. The results would be a disastrous, explosive decompression.

Yamun and his people were busy up front. Carter slipped out of his seat and grabbed the big gun from the dead Arab's hand.

It was a pellet gun. Everything was made of plastic, and it looked very much like the handle of an umbrella. It was how they got their weapons past security.

Carter turned and started up the aisle just as one of

Yamun's women and one of the men appeared from around the center bulkhead.

Carter fired twice in rapid succession before either of them had a chance to raise their weapons. The first shot hit the woman in the chest, and the second hit the man in the throat.

They both staggered back, and Carter leaned forward, pulling out his stiletto.

The passengers were screaming hysterically now. Some of them had leaped out into the aisle, covering Carter's movements.

Anita had gotten out of her seat and was right behind Carter as he leaped on the man who had brought up his gun. Carter drove the blade of his stiletto up between the man's ribs, piercing his heart, while he deflected the barrel of the man's gun with the plastic pellet gun in his left hand.

The Arab was down. Carter grabbed the gun and gave it to Anita.

"Yamun, his woman, and the other man are still forward," he shouted to Anita over the noise.

They started forward, shoving people out of the way. One large man, wearing cowboy boots, turned around and tried to grab Anita. Carter sidestepped him, shifted the bloody stiletto to his gun hand, and clipped the man neatly on the jaw. The Texan fell back over a couple in their seats.

The speed indicator over the forward bulkhead read Mach 1.6. They were still accelerating.

Two flight attendants lay dead in the aisle near the front galley. As Carter was stepping over them, Yamun's woman came around the corner, her pistol up. She fired, the shot hitting Carter in the left arm, just below his elbow.

Carter popped off a shot, and Anita fired from behind him. Both shots hit the woman. She fell back, blood streaming from two holes in her chest, both just below her left breast.

The door to the flight deck was closed. Carter leaped forward, and an instant later something very hard slammed into his side, knocking him off his feet, the gun slipping from his grasp.

He scrambled around, the stiletto still in his left hand, his fingers stiff and nearly without feeling because of his wound.

Yamun stood there, just by the galley, a maniacal grin on his face. He was a tall man, with thick shoulders and a square, almost handsome face. He looked powerful. He held one of the large plastic pistols in his hand.

"Now it is too late," he said. "Now you die." He was back around the corner, and Anita could not get a clear shot. People were screaming and pushing, trying to get out of the way.

The door to the flight deck opened, and a man stepped out. He held a gun.

"No!" Yamun shouted, half turning his way.

Anita fired twice, the first shot hitting the man in the chest, the second in his face, shoving him backward into the flight deck.

Yamun roared with rage. He spun around the corner and fired five shots in quick succession at Anita, each one hitting her, driving her backward into the panic-stricken passengers.

Carter leaped up, shifting the stiletto to his right hand, and charged into Yamun, who was turning back.

The Mach indicator overhead chimed to 2.0, and the automatic pilot leveled them off, directly on course for Washington, D.C.

Carter and Yamun went crashing back into the galley, the razor-sharp stiletto slicing the muscles and nerves above Yamun's left elbow.

Like an enraged bull, the Arab terrorist shoved Carter aside and fired point-blank, the shot hitting Carter's left calf. He pulled the trigger again, but nothing happened. The weapon was empty.

Yamun threw the heavy gun at Carter, the butt striking Carter in the temple before he could duck, his head bouncing against the stainless steel cabinet behind him, stars and spots suddenly before his eyes.

Yamun charged, his huge, meaty fist appearing as if out of nowhere.

Carter managed to turn enough so that the blow was deflected, Yamun's fist slamming into the cabinet.

Carter brought the stiletto up and in, but Yamun had been a fighter for too long. The Arab twisted his body out of the way, the blade penetrating his skin but sliding off the hip-bone.

Yamun had Carter's knife hand, and he bent it backward with relative ease. His strength was incredible. There was an intense fire in his dark eyes, and an insane grin on his lips.

"Now you will die, Carter," he hissed.

Carter's right wrist snapped, the sickening pain screaming through his body, the knife falling to the floor, his head suddenly clearing, everything instantly becoming crystal-clear to him.

He brought his right knee up into Yamun's groin, putting every ounce of strength he had into it.

The big Arab reared back, the air rushing out of him in one belch.

Carter scrambled over, snatching up his stiletto with his left hand, blood streaming down from the wound in his arm, his fingers all but useless.

Yamun turned back to him, his eyes pinpoints of venomous hate, and swung his fist.

At that instant Carter lunged forward, driving the stiletto to the hilt into the big man's chest, blood gushing everywhere.

Yamun was shoved backward by the sheer force of the blow. He did not get back up.

Carter crawled over to him. Yamun's eyes were open, his mouth working, trying to form words.

"Miram . . ." he whispered. "You killed her!" Then he died.

Carter looked at him. "No," he said. "You did."

He crawled painfully back to where Anita lay. She too was dead. The front of her dress was covered in blood. He gently closed her eyes.

The passengers were beginning to calm down. They looked at him.

Carter turned and went up to the flight deck. The SST was on automatic pilot. The pilot, the copilot, and the navigator were all dead. They had been shot in the head with the plastic pistols.

The Concorde, after all, is nothing but an airplane, somewhat more complicated than average, but an airplane just the same.

By the time they had crossed the Atlantic, Carter's wounds had been bandaged, he had received some instructions over the radio from Washington air traffic control, and they came in for a landing . . . not as smooth as it could have been, but on time.

EPILOGUE

It was the end of a beautiful September before Carter was fit to travel again, though he still was not ready for a new assignment.

The President had presented him with a letter of commendation, classified top-secret, of course. It wouldn't do to advertise just how vulnerable the President and the entire government of the United States were, or how close Yamun had come.

Carter requested and was given a thirty-day leave, and before he left, Hawk asked where he was going.

"I thought I'd go over to Monaco," Carter said.

"Israel first?"

Carter smiled and nodded. "There's someone there, I think, who needs an explanation."

"Have a good vacation," Hawk said.

Carter took the Paris flight out that same night, and then in the morning took the El Al flight direct to Tel Aviv.

He was not stopped at customs, nor was he delayed leaving the city in his rented Ford. David Lapides certainly was not going to thank him for finally eliminating Yamun, but he wasn't going to hinder Carter for it either.

The weather was absolutely perfect, the early afternoon

warm and pleasant as he drove up into the hills, the citrus trees giving way to the gnarled olive orchards.

He arrived at the Gan Har 'Evm kibbutz a few minutes before two o'clock, parked in front of the administration building, and went in.

Katy Shwartz was there. She looked up and smiled. But there was a sadness to it. "You're back," she said, rising from her desk.

Carter nodded. "Is he . . ."

She shook her head. "Peri Sharon died two weeks ago," she said.

"He knew about Yamun?"

"Yes," she said. She came around the desk to him and took his arm. She seemed to have aged in the few months since Carter had seen her last. She was no longer a young girl. She was a woman now. A dark-haired beauty.

They went outside.

"He said that when you returned, I was to tell you that he understood about Miram Yamun. And that it was for the best, the way it had turned out. There had been too much hate inside her . . . hate that had buried whatever love she might once have been capable of."

"Peri talked to you a lot."

"He was my uncle. It's why I came over here in the first place. He had no one else."

Carter nodded. He looked toward the hills. It was very pleasant here. For the moment, peaceful.

"You look awful," Katy said.

Carter turned back and smiled. "That's how I feel."

She looked appraisingly at him. "Are you on vacation . . . or recuperative leave, or something?"

"Or something," he said.

She laughed. "The invitation is still open. There's lots of work to be done here, but I make a mean chicken soup."

"No commitments," Carter said, feeling like a heel for saying it.

"Not on your life," she said. "I'll be damned if I'll get involved with someone like my uncle who runs around the world getting himself shot up." She laughed again. "But for a week or two it might be fun."

DON'T MISS THE NEXT NEW
NICK CARTER SPY THRILLER

LAST FLIGHT TO MOSCOW

"Nick, there's someone outside! Nick, please wake up! There are men in the yard and one crawling up—Nick!"

Tammi's voice came to him as a dream that was quickly turning into a nightmare. Normally, Nick Carter needed only the snap of a twig or the cocking of a pistol hammer to bring him from deep sleep to instant alertness. But the toll on his energies had been formidable for too long. He was drained.

"Prowlers," he murmured, half in his sleep. "Anybody as beautiful as you must have prowlers and peeping-Toms galore. Go back to sleep."

"Nick," Tammi snapped, shaking his muscular shoulder, "prowlers and peeping-Toms don't come at the crack of dawn. There are men with guns outside—and they're coming in one way or another!"

That did it. Men with guns. Carter didn't know how they had tracked him here, but he had no doubt that the men were part of Anatoly Gritchkin's bodyguard. He lunged from the bed and started to tape Pierre to his thigh when he heard glass shatter in a downstairs room.

Tammi started to scream, but Carter quickly had his hand over her mouth. "Don't make a sound. This is a big house and we have the advantage. They don't know where we are." He laid the gas bomb on a dresser and put on his holster with Wilhelmina tucked inside.

"Who are they? What do they want?"

He saw no reason to lie for her protection. "They're Russian spies, KGB—and they're after me."

"Why?"

"It's complicated." He was slipping into his trousers when they heard a board squeak somewhere down below. Outside on the roof, something went scuttling down the tiles and crashed with a muffled sound on the ground.

"Oh my God," Tammi cried. "They're all over the place."

"Yeah. Look, I want you to get into that dressing room and lock the door. It has no windows, so you'll be safe there. Please, don't even try to argue. We have no time." He was fully dressed now, with his Luger and stiletto in place under his arm and on his wrist. He ushered the lovely woman toward the dressing room. "I may have to mess up your pad a little. With luck, nothing important will be destroyed."

"My Renoir," she cried, trying to break away from him.

"Go to the den," Carter warned her, "and it'll be your cute little derriere instead of a painting of one. Please, stay in the dressing room until I tell our callers we aren't interested in whatever it is they're selling."

"What *are* they selling, Nick?"

"Terror, then death. Get cracking, girl." Even as Carter gently slapped her buttocks to move her along, he heard stair treads squeak and knew that two heavy men were coming up. The man out on the roof was silent after having blown his cover by knocking a loose tile to the ground. That accounted for three men. Carter was thinking of the five men who had gone with the spy on that crazy round-robin ride. If they were assigned to him, then all five would likely be along on this mission.

With Tammi locked in the dressing room, Carter moved to a front window and surveyed the dark lawn below. The sky was brightening by the minute, but the cluster of trees on Tammi's lawn cast deep shadows and kept it pre-dawn in the yard. Even so, Carter spotted a telltale cloud of smoke that could have been fog flowing gently out from behind a large elm tree. He watched and, sure enough, the man behind the tree leaned out for a quick glimpse of the house. He was looking for a signal from one of the men inside or the man on the roof. No signal was forthcoming, so he ducked back behind the tree and took another drag on his cigarette.

Carter scanned the rest of the yard and saw the next man—the fifth in the group—crouched behind the green Volvo in the driveway. The man himself was completely out of sight, but his brown shoes showed from beneath the front bumper in a kind of lump that Carter knew was not part of the automobile.

He made a quick decision to take the man on the roof first. He recalled Tammi's house had a large attic. He found the narrow staircase leading to it and went up, Luger in hand. The attic was empty, but there were tiny windows in the dormers. Carter went to the one nearest the area where they'd heard the loose tile scuttle down. He slid up the window and looked out. The side and back yards were clear of KGB agents. Carter was certain he had made the locations of all the men, and that the kill party consisted of the five who had gone joyriding with Gritchkin last night.

Carter eased out onto the roof and peered around the dormer toward the peak. He saw the Russian's hands on the ridge tiles and knew that the man was lying on his stomach on the opposite slope of the roof. The man was still keeping a low profile after his clumsiness with the tile. Carter moved slowly up the roof, his dark eyes constantly on the hands that gripped the ridge ten feet above.

He stopped five feet short of the peak and put away the Luger. Silence was necessary unless he wanted the other four to zero in on him. He flicked the stiletto into his right hand

and went the remaining distance. He sat on the smooth tiles just below the ridge.

"Is that you, Comrade Stanislav?" he whispered in excellent Muscovite Russian.

"No, I'm Krumpinsky," the man whispered back. "Are you Salizar?"

"Yes. Lie still. I'm coming over."

"Watch out for loose tiles," Krumpinsky said hoarsely and contritely. "I found one with my foot. I suppose you heard the results."

"I heard."

Now that the man was off his guard, Carter slid over the ridge as swiftly as he could, his back to Krumpinsky. Once he was beside the man, he swung with the stiletto and dealt him a lethal blow just below the rib cage. The sharp blade punctured a kidney, and Carter twisted the needlelike instrument quickly to make certain the man didn't linger in pain.

Krumpinsky died with a soft moan on his lips. When his body went slack and his hands released their grip on the ridge, Carter pinned him to the roof with strong arms, then eased him down to where two sections of roof angled together. He settled the dead agent in the crotch of the roof, then retraced his steps to the attic window.

Returning to the second floor, Carter saw one man sneaking into the master bedroom where Tammi was locked in. If the KGB man, whom Carter recognized from the airport, shot off the lock, Tammi would be easy pickings.

Carter had to avoid that. He was kneeling and taking aim on the man when he caught movement from his left. The second man, who had come through the downstairs window, was now emerging from a spare bedroom. The man saw Carter and raised his weapon. Carter swung around and shot the man on his left, who fired his revolver at the same time, but missed.

The discharge of the heavy Luger and the revolver in the confined space was like a bomb thrown into a sealed vault. The man fell, clutching his chest where the 9mm slug had crashed through muscles and bones and into his heart. He rolled to his back and blood pumped like a gusher up through his shirt.

Carter was already looking down the long corridor. The man who had been at Tammi's door was gone. Carter knew he was inside the bedroom. He had to bring him out of there before the two outside men came barging in. Unless they were deaf, the sound of Wilhelmina alone must have set them into action. In fact, Carter mused, the roar of the Luger must have awakened the whole damn neighborhood. Soon, he guessed, he'd hear the irritating siren of a Dutch police car.

For now, the silence in the house seemed deafening to Carter. He listened for the men outside to come in, but heard no activity downstairs. He listened for sounds from Tammi's bedroom. Nothing there. He went slowly down the hall, inching along the wall, the Luger leading the way in his strong grip.

Time was leaping at him now. He had to flush the KGB man out of Tammi's room before the man discovered the locked dressing room and before the outside men became inside men. He couldn't rush though. His only chance was to surprise the man in Tammi's room. The Russian wouldn't know for certain whether his own man or the American was dead out in the corridor. He'd have to opt for the worst, and that meant he was now seeking a hiding place in the big pink bedroom.

The only hiding place was the dressing room . . .

—From LAST FLIGHT TO MOSCOW
A New Nick Carter Spy Thriller
From Charter in June 1985

☐ 74965-8	SAN JUAN INFERNO	$2.50
☐ 79073-9	THE STRONTIUM CODE	$2.50
☐ 82726-8	TURKISH BLOODBATH	$2.25
☐ 14220-6	DEATH ISLAND	$2.50
☐ 95935-0	ZERO-HOUR STRIKE FORCE	$2.50
☐ 03223-0	ASSIGNMENT: RIO	$2.50
☐ 14222-2	DEATH HAND PLAY	$2.50
☐ 29782-X	THE GOLDEN BULL	$2.50
☐ 45520-4	THE KREMLIN KILL	$2.50
☐ 52276-9	THE MAYAN CONNECTION	$2.50
☐ 10561-0	CIRCLE OF SCORPIONS	$2.50
☐ 06861-8	THE BLUE ICE AFFAIR	$2.50
☐ 51353-0	THE MACAO MASSACRE	$2.50
☐ 69180-3	PURSUIT OF THE EAGLE	

Prices may be slightly higher in Canada.

Available at your local bookstore or return this form to:

 CHARTER BOOKS
Book Mailing Service
P.O. Box 690, Rockville Centre, NY 11571

Please send me the titles checked above. I enclose _____ Include 75¢ for postage and handling if one book is ordered; 25¢ per book for two or more not to exceed $1.75. California, Illinois, New York and Tennessee residents please add sales tax.

NAME_____

ADDRESS_____

CITY_____ STATE/ZIP_____

(allow six weeks for delivery.)

A8